LOST
in
KOOTZNOO
WOO

Kathleen Morris

<u>Lost in Kootznoowoo</u>

The Fatherless Series - Book 1

By Kathleen Morris

Amazon Paperback Edition
Copyright 2025 by Kathleen Morris
Rouge Publishing

ISBN: 978-1-927828-63-2

Table of Contents

Dedication
This book is dedicated to my own ginger Boone.
You know who you are!

FRESH RAIN

Adventure, that's what she needed.

Kelly wiped her tears as she finalized her online purchase.

She was going to Alaska.

Alone!

Do people even do that anymore?

She sure hoped so, because she just put all her savings down on a non-refundable cruise. No turning back now.

And no dumb boyfriend to have to worry about.

For the longest time, Kelly had her suspicions about him. It wasn't even about how he ended it with her. It wasn't even the fact that he never wanted to go anywhere. It was the fact that he didn't want to go anywhere with *her*.

All those mysterious *work* calls. All those excuses. All those lies right in front of her nose. He was a mastermind at deception, and she was the dummy for believing him for so long.

Well, not anymore.

Today marked the start of a new life. For the first time in a long time, Kelly felt free of his narcissistic ways. If it hadn't been for the fact that she saw him with that woman, he never would have sent her the insulting text that ended their relationship.

Who breaks up by text anyway?

A coward! A cheater! That's who!

Well, good riddance, *Ted!*

The soft June rain speckled against Kelly's apartment window as she saw her reflection in it. Her tears matched the raindrops as they streamed down one by one. Why was she crying for that idiot?

I thought I was in love.

How damaged she must be to think a man like that was genuine. When it came to men, she sure knew how to pick 'em.

Kelly blamed that on the first man who ever let her down. Her dad! He left her when she was three, and she's replayed those abandonment issues over and over in her mind ever since. It's no wonder she can't seem to find a good man. They don't exist.

She rubbed her eyes and blew her nose again.

Stop it, Kelly! He doesn't deserve your tears.

As the rain started to let up, Kelly recognized her new beginning lay right in front of her. It smelled like lilacs and maple trees, and mouldy suitcases she hadn't used in years.

She stuffed her suitcase with just about everything she owned, right down to her favourite novel. Maybe she'd get to read it on the ship. She hadn't been able to do that in a long time. She was always working.

When she asked her boss for some time off, she told her it was about time. Kelly hadn't had a vacation in years. In fact, all she ever did was work. It's how she dealt with pain, and pain seemed like the only thing that was ever consistent in her life.

How pathetic!

There were so many things in her life she wished were different. She didn't really have any friends. Whose fault was that when all she ever did was work? Kelly knew she had to make changes, but she didn't know how to go about doing that.

All she knew how to do was suck it up.

That's all Ted ever told her to do. It was like he had no heart. He just wrote her feelings off like she didn't matter. She was used to that. She realized she let him bulldoze over her too many times.

Why?

What was wrong with her? She shouldn't have let their relationship go on so long. He was mean to her most of the time, but she just took it. Even her co-workers tried to warn her, but she didn't listen.

Maybe she was broken somehow.

If that was the case, she had no clue how to fix herself.

Even therapy didn't work. Her therapist told her she had a father wound that was affecting her relationships, whatever that meant.

Kelly hated him telling her this.

Ted was the way he was, and it wasn't her fault. Why blame her? He was a jerk, and that had nothing to do with her.

She stuffed her suitcase while throwing insults at him as if he were right there. She wished she could tell him these things to his face. One day she would, but not now. Right now, she just wanted to get out of there.

She wanted to go anywhere but there.

Alaska was that place. It had to be. Anything was better than this rotten city with all its bad memories.

Kelly looked at her watch and hurried with her packing. She realized she didn't need everything she packed, but it was better to be safe than sorry. Who knew what the weather would be like there? She'd never been to the ocean.

She'd never been on a cruise. She'd never been anywhere.

It was exciting. Who knew what adventure awaited her there? She was sure it was what she needed. It was the perfect way to deal with the breakup. She wasn't even sure she wanted to live in the same city as Ted anymore.

Maybe if she liked Alaska, she'd stay.

But she moved so many times, and none of them ever worked out. She went through so many bad breakups and moved so many times. She burned too many bridges, all because of the deadbeat losers she dated. She was absolutely sick of it!

At this point, Kelly didn't think she could ever love again.

Maybe she wasn't capable.

All she knew was that she had to get out of there. Escaping was the only solution. Taking a trip was just what she needed to get her bearings straight. It had to be. She had nothing left.

Going alone was risky, though. Not that she was afraid to be alone. She was used to that. She was a loner all her life. It was the other part that was difficult. The part that required her to be vulnerable with people. Making friends was her handicap. She hoped she was up for the challenge.

It was time for a new start. It was time for excitement. It was time to leave the painful memories behind. Maybe she wouldn't even come back. *That was a thought.*

Whales. Bears. Mother Nature. Maybe they had something in store for her. *The Alaskan wilderness awaits.* She could hardly contain her excitement. This adventure was about to begin.

Alaska, here I come!

THE PRACTICE

Kelly didn't get out much. Even when she was seeing Ted, they rarely went anywhere. Booking a flight was not second nature to her. By mistake, she booked a non-connecting flight to Vancouver and suffered the whole way there.

She thought she had booked Toronto to Vancouver non-stop, but to her surprise, she had a layover in Saskatoon. That put her behind several hours, which meant she was probably going to be late boarding the ship.

According to cruise rules, if you miss the scheduled boarding time, they won't let you board. That meant you can't go. Non-refundable kept running through her mind.

The airline was low-budget as well, which added unwanted stress to the journey. Under her breath, she vowed never to fly on *Where Airlines* ever again. They squashed people in like sardines. They sat on the tarmac for three excruciating hours without air conditioning as maintenance tried to get the navigation working.

It was shocking that the airline was so unreliable.

Regardless, Kelly was bound and determined not to let this setback ruin her excitement. After all, she had done it. She was going to Alaska. A cruise was just the adventure she was looking for, and she could hardly wait to escape.

In Kelly's mind, she knew going solo would be a challenge, but that wasn't stopping her. She even brushed up on her communication skills by talking to everyone she met. *Almost.*

"Lady, can you get moving, please?"

The old lady with her hands on her hips told her she was holding up the line. The truth of the matter was, Kelly was finishing a conversation with a college professor she met on the plane. He was a lovely old gentleman.

She was practicing.

"I'm sorry, ma'am," Kelly apologized as she went through the gate at the Vancouver airport. They had finally arrived, and it was almost time to board the ship. She couldn't believe she made it on time. Just barely!

Somehow, she had to get from the terminal to the ship in less than an hour. Luckily, there was a shuttle. She ran to it and pounded on the side of the bus. It was just about to pull away when the doors opened.

"Thank you, sir!" she panted out of breath. "You don't know how much this means!" She dragged her carry-on up the stairs with her purse in hand and found one of the last seats available on the bus.

Kelly was grateful to have made it on time. She was lucky to get a seat. She sat across from a young couple, visibly in love. How ironic. They cuddled and groped each other like teenagers. They practically were. "How long have you been together?" she smiled.

"We just got married," the woman beamed. "We met three years ago and instantly fell in love. When you know, you know!" They both giggled.

Lovely! That's how long she and Ted were together. Why didn't it work out that way for her?

For some reason, she felt like love was meant for everyone else but her. She seemed to attract deadbeats and cheaters. *Joy.*

Kelly gulped hard and tried to stop herself from tearing up. Her face flushed as it started to overheat. Was this another panic attack?

"Are you okay, miss?"

Miss? Don't remind me.

"I'm fine. Sorry, it was a long trip." Kelly could hear them asking her more questions, but her mind drifted. Her thoughts brought her back to her decision to travel solo. Maybe it was a mistake after all. She didn't expect to feel like this.

They continued talking to her, though she couldn't make out a word of it. It made her head spin and her skin sweaty and red. A panic attack for sure. Now what was she going to do? Her doctor told her to remember to breathe.

Deep, slow breathing... One. Two. Three. What do you see? The people. The seats. The windows of the bus. Her brown purse. Her carry-on. It was taking up space in the aisle while other people had luggage on their laps.

Then, suddenly, as if startled out of a stupor, she realized something was missing. *Her luggage.* She had left the other two suitcases at the airport.

What was she going to do now?

It was because she was so hyper-focused on talking to people at the airport that she forgot her luggage. This was *stupid!* Why did she think she had to do all this practicing?

With everything that had happened so far, she wondered if she should just turn around and go home. For a moment, looking at all the strangers on the bus, reality kicked in.

She had never felt so alone.

THE MISTAKE

Boone started down the wrong path just after finishing college. Truth be told, if he could turn back the clock, there were a lot of things he'd do differently. For one, he wouldn't have trusted his buddy Jimmy.

Even Southeastern Alaska had its criminals, and Jimmy was one of them. His persuasive personality drew people to him for many reasons, most of them illegal.

"Just help me out this one time, Boone!"

"No!"

"C'mon, buddy, all you gotta do is use that old plane of yours. A grand in your pocket for flying it to Anchorage is all I'm asking."

"Fine!" Boone whispered, "Just this once." After all, he could use the money.

Against his better judgment, Boone made the worst mistake of his life. He transported stolen goods for his buddy on the old float plane his father left him. The old man willed it to him after he died in a car accident. He drove drunk one too many times.

Bad judgment seemed to run in his family.

Boone squinted in the warm June sun as he tried to shake the memories. He'd only been out of prison for a year now, but it was hard to make a comeback. Thankfully, a family friend kept the old plane in storage, but for some reason, he thought it was in better condition than that.

What an old rust bucket.

He'd have to put his schooling to work. At least he still had that, even though he never got to complete a full apprenticeship. He lost that when he went to jail.

Shake it, Boone! The memories kept flooding in, but he was still glad to be back home, even though the last year had been a wash. Maybe he could finally make a go of his guided tour business this season. Tourism was lucrative in Juneau, with plenty of cruise ships bringing in customers.

He figured, since his AME apprenticeship was in the toilet, he had to go to plan B. He still knew his stuff, and he could turn any old piece of junk into a solid flying machine. Combining his two skills was a perfect match.

He'll fly them in himself, and maintain the float plane too. A one-man show. Then he'll guide them through Tlingit territory. *Fortress of the Bears.* His mother's ancestors came from there. Her indigenous roots meant more to Boone than his drunk of a father's Scottish blood.

He sure wished he looked more like his mother. Then he wouldn't see his father's ugly face every time he looked in the mirror. Boone blamed his father's drinking for most of his problems. If it wasn't for his dysfunctional upbringing, maybe he wouldn't have done what he did.

But then, he had nobody to blame but himself. That's what he learned in therapy anyway. He was accountable for his actions.

I chose to break the law.

It was an embarrassment, really. He knew better. He stayed away from alcohol. He swore he'd never be a drunk like his old man. He even stayed away from drugs. Never in a million years had he thought about being a thief, yet that's what he had become.

For what? A friend? Why?

And where was Jimmy now?

Though Boone's Class E felony landed him two years in Goose Creek Correctional, Jimmy was the big fish. They gave him 5 years at Spring Creek. No place he ever wanted to go. The stories coming out of there were horrifying.

Last he heard, Jimbo knifed some guy there and got convicted of manslaughter. No doubt, self-defence, but that's what happens there.

It was bad enough at Goose Creek. His stay was no picnic either. Yet, something happened to him there, and he's not talking about the tattoos. He knew better about that, too, but learned his lesson the hard way after getting a staph infection and nearly losing his life over it.

Yet, it was still worth it. They told his story.

Boone looked down at the multiple tattoos up and down both arms, depicting what happened to him there. He smiled and remembered it was there that he experienced the most profound grace and forgiveness one man could ever know.

It's where he found Jesus.

Boone remembered what rock bottom felt like. It was there, when he had nothing left, that Christ met him where he was at. Such a tender grace for an unworthy man like him.

And why him? Boone could think of several guys who were more cleaned up than he was. But then, he figured, that's not how it works.

We all fall short of the glory of God. That's why we all need Him.

So many guys in prison stayed at rock bottom, even when they got out. He was fortunate to get a second chance. That's why he decided to name his business that.

Of all the things he could have done after being released, he chose to come back to his roots. He was still shaking his head at that one. Thankfully, he had the opportunity. Most ex-cons don't.

His Aunt Sally made sure he was taken care of. She always told him, "Remember who you are. You are a child of the King! The devil can't touch you!"

She was a devout believer ever since his mom's passing. She went to church all her life, but never had a relationship with Jesus, until a few years ago. He was told she and her prayer team had prayed for him the whole time he was in prison.

She had such a great heart and loved him dearly. He would have been more than happy to move to Angoon and stay with her, but it didn't seem like the right fit. At least not now.

Juneau was his choice.

He didn't think he could make a go of his business without being near the cruise ships. The only other option was flying thirty minutes across the wilderness from Angoon to Juneau every time he had a tour. That would've been fine with him, but the unpredictable weather wasn't.

No, God brought him to Juneau for a reason.

He didn't know what it was yet, other than business, but he figured God would reveal it soon enough. Now he'd better get at it. This work wasn't going to get done by itself.

He still had a lot to do.

BE STILL

Put them over there!" Boone told the two young boys he hired to stock the old red and white float plane while he worked on the engine.

It was almost ready to fly.

June meant the bears were at their peak mating season, which meant it was the best time to guide. The increased bear activity made his job of sighting them a whole lot easier. Hopefully, he didn't have any trouble in that regard. People pay good money to see them, and when they don't show up, it's bad for business. Not that he could control any of that.

"Did you load both totes?" he asked the boys before they headed off the seaplane dock.

"We did it all, boss."

"Just checking," Boone laughed at himself. He didn't realize how nervous he was. This new venture had to be successful. He put every dime into the business. *It will work!* Not like his dad ran it. *He was sober.*

He was responsible.

Granted, Boone was the convict, but even still, anything was better than his dad's mismanaged embarrassment of a guiding business. How many times as a teenager did he have to take over the guide because his dad was too intoxicated to finish it?

Thank the Lord his old man never piloted the plane. He always hired help until Boone got his pilot's license. After that, he had to both fly the plane and help his dad guide.

It was no wonder the business didn't do well. Thankfully, he escaped most of the chaos when he went to school to be an aircraft mechanic. Boone was also thankful for the small inheritance his mother left him so he could further his education. Had it not been for her, he would have ended up like his father.

Yet, there he was.

Boone cleared his throat and took a breath. *Sorry mom! I tried.* He couldn't help but feel like he let her down somehow. She had such high hopes for him to be a licensed AME before she died. She wanted him to have a way out, and look what he did with it.

Man, all these memories. Why couldn't he shake them?

It was times like these that Boone wished his mother were still alive. He particularly missed their endless phone conversations. She always listened to every little problem he had.

Cancer took her way too young.

Bitterness started to creep in again. *It's your fault!* Boone always blamed his father. *Your stupid drinking made Mom sick!*

The year he finished AME, he came back home to confront his dad about it. Boone remembered the words that haunted him. *You killed her, Dad! YOU did it! You and your stupid drinking drove Mom to the grave!*

How was Boone supposed to know his dad would drink himself into a stupor that night and meet face to face with a moose?

Enough!

These memories were getting him nowhere. It was time to stop! It was time to heal! It was time to forgive. He knew that. Yet...this place, this plane...they brought it all back. Emotions threw him back and forth just like the pontoons against the tide.

He knew he should let it all go, but there were some things he had a hard time with. *Blame.* He blamed himself for both of his parents' deaths. If he hadn't shouted obscenities at his father that day, maybe he'd still be alive. Accusing him of causing his mother's cancer was a terrible thing to do, even if it was true.

Did he cause his father to deliberately drive into a moose, or was that just a coincidence? He didn't really have an answer. Only God knew. Yet, he knew God forgave him of everything, not just some things.

The guilt was still real, though. But, like his aunt kept telling him, "Remember who you are. You are a child of the King. The devil can't touch you."

Yeah, he knew it, but he still had a hard time. He realized he should stop. He let that monster destroy his soul long enough. Still, it seemed to have such a hold on him.

Indirectly, he blamed himself for his mother's death, too. If he had been stronger, she might not have gotten sick. He could have insisted that his father go to rehab. He could have helped his mom get help dealing with him. He could have brought his mother to a shelter instead of being a selfish teenager.

He should have stopped the drunken bum!

Forgive!

I know, Lord, I'm trying.

Boone moved his wrench as he tightened a few bolts in the engine. *There! That should do it.* He wiped his greasy hands and closed the cowling, hoping his mind would stop reeling now.

"You gotta stop blaming yourself, Boone!" Aunt Sally told him one night when he beat himself up about it. "It's not your fault. You were just a kid. He was to blame. *Only him!*"

In his heart, he knew that, but his mind kept telling him otherwise. He decided to stop, close his eyes, and just listen to the harbour noise. He remembered what he was taught. When he got like this, he needed to take a moment and breathe.

Boone knew the spiritual side of that therapy now. All he had to do was remember that God was in control, not him. There's nothing He doesn't see. There's nothing He doesn't have a handle on. In fact, it reminded him of one of his favourite verses, one he repeated often in prison.

It was from the book of Job. That book fascinated him. He read it over and over during his incarceration. If someone like Job could make it through the hell he had endured, so could he.

And one day, all that the enemy had stolen from him will be restored. *"He will once again fill your mouth with laughter, and your lips with shouts of joy."*

Boone didn't know what it was about that verse, but it brought tears to his eyes every time he read it. He knew that was the truth, not the lies the devil was feeding him.

As he watched the waves rise and fall in the emerald waterfront, he inhaled the salty air and knew it was God speaking to him. Like always, when he finally stopped to listen, Boone could hear His gentle voice in the ocean breeze.

Be still and know that I am God

SAY GOODBYE

I t was happening.

The oversized cruise ship inched toward the Vancouver harbour, pushing forward like a rite of passage. Kelly felt like a queen as she sucked in the salty June air, ready for the adventure that awaited her.

The late-day sun warmed her face as they headed to sea. Icebergs and picturesque mountains awaited the new adventure she found herself on. It was a long time coming, this freedom, this sense of independence.

Why didn't she do it earlier?

For twenty-five years of her life, she'd lived a subservient lifestyle, just accepting whatever came along, giving her power away. It was almost as if she didn't matter. Perhaps that's why she ended up with Ted. Perhaps that's why she went through so many men. Better yet, that's why they went through her.

"Pretty, isn't it?" Kelly spoke to the man next to her, deciding to be bold. She thought he was alone too for a moment, but then saw him holding hands with a short brunette beside him.

"He's taken, honey!" the woman smirked. She pulled the man to another vantage point against the side of the ship, far away from her.

Sheesh! This is going to be harder than I thought.

Shrugging, Kelly moved to the loungers on the deck of the ship and stretched out to relax. The ship had many places to rest. It was gigantic. Never had she been on a boat so huge. It didn't even resemble a boat when you were on it. It felt more like a floating resort or a mini city.

By the time they fully left the harbour, the captain welcomed them by intercom. He advised all passengers to meet on the promenade deck for a safety lesson.

Kelly inched forward through the crowd and went to her assigned location. In the crowd, she felt alone, but tried to make small talk with all the excited passengers as best she could.

"What are those patches behind your ears?" she asked the lady in front of her. They were all wearing them.

"I beg your pardon?" the lady seemed annoyed.

"I asked you, what are those patches behind your ears?"

"Seasickness patches."

The moment Kelly was told what they were, her jaw dropped. *Seasickness patches.* Everyone had them on. "How do you get them?"

After multiple people joined in the conversation, she felt embarrassed that she didn't know. They told her it was a prescription from the doctor. Turns out you had to start wearing the patch a few days before setting sail so you don't get seasick.

"Seriously? You didn't know that?"

They looked at her as if she were a dummy. She had no idea such a thing even existed. She supposed that's what she got for booking a last-minute cruise. Kelly feared her inexperience would get the best of her.

I guess I'd better get used to puking!

Trying to put the uncomfortable thought aside, Kelly focused on the beaming warm sunshine. Its cascading energy illuminated the deck of the ship like a halo. Had she made a mistake going on this trip? Could she find happiness as a solo traveller?

Maybe.

Yet, there she was, feeling sorry for herself, trying to make the best of a difficult situation. Wasn't that what she'd done her entire life?

As far back as she could remember, Kelly had a different way of seeing things. Some would say she wore rose coloured glasses. If that was the case, she wore them proudly. Why? Because that's all she had.

Happiness was not plentiful when you didn't have a father

like everyone else. You learned quickly that in order to be happy, you had to pretend you were normal. In reality, you weren't. You were just weird.

Growing up, Kelly remembered being made fun of whenever Father's Day came around. "We're making Father's Day cards today, class," her teacher would say.

"But I don't have a dad."

"How can you not have a dad?" her friends laughed and teased. "Everyone has a dad."

Yet, for Kelly, it was a void she couldn't explain. It was a pain she couldn't remove. As a child, all she wanted was her daddy to come home, but he never did. The abandonment she felt plagued her throughout her entire life.

Even now.

This sadness felt like part of the journey somehow. She couldn't tell if it was good or bad, but one thing was clear: Travelling by herself seemed to open up old, familiar wounds. At the airport. The layover. Boarding the ship. It was an unbelievable loneliness. She could scream in the middle of a crowd and still feel invisible.

Why?

Perhaps it really was a mistake to go on this trip alone. So far, the experience has not been enjoyable. Was she going to have to get off at the next port and fly home early?

But I don't want to!

Something inside of her wanted her to fight, to try, to give it another chance. Yet, the other side of her said, *Run, run like you always do!* That, she had no problem with. She had run away from difficult situations all her life. But stay? That was the hard part.

Regardless, this trip seemed to be an odd therapy of sorts. It seemed to be resurfacing pain she'd buried for a long time. Then, force her to say goodbye to it once and for all, even though she didn't want to.

Phycology. It's a strange beast.

Now, with the enormity of the ship, she realized just how

alone she really was, and she definitely did not like that feeling. She tried to say hi to as many people as she could, riding off into the sunset, but it was severely awkward.

Why did socializing always have to feel forced?

It had been like that for far too long. Kelly hoped the trip would get her out of her shell. This was her chance. If Ted could see her now, he wouldn't believe it. He always teased her that she was too shy.

He was a big part of the problem, though.

Yet, she was shy. She was the quieter type who sat in the corner and didn't say a word. A wallflower, perhaps. She called herself a late bloomer.

Well, Kelly, it was time to bloom!

TAKE THE PILL

Morning came early as it shone through the small porthole in her room. Kelly stood up on her bed, teetering as she pushed herself up to see. The rise and fall of the ocean was something she'd never seen before. *How beautiful!*

This was worth it after all.

She pressed her warm cheeks against the cold glass window and watched the waves go up and down. *Up and down.* It was hypnotizing.

Breakfast was being served, but she wanted to take in the sea for a little bit longer before heading out. When would she ever see this spectacular view again? The open water was like a whole new world. She wanted to look at it as long as she could.

That was a mistake.

Up and down, and up and down. It was no longer mesmerizing but sickening. It started turning her stomach the longer she looked at it.

Uh oh!

Queasiness started taking over.

Quickly, she pulled herself away from the porthole and felt dizzy. *It will pass*, she told herself as she grabbed her door pass and headed to breakfast. *It will pass!*

The endless buffet was remarkable! Every breakfast option imaginable appeared on numerous tables, including a dietary restriction area. That would be her section for the rest of the trip. Kelly was thankful for that.

She could see French toast, waffles, and pancakes. All versions she could eat. There was a meat table with scrambled eggs and bacon, ham, beef, chicken and fish. For the vegetarian, there were tables of fresh fruits and vegetables. It was an amazing sight to see!

If her stomach allowed it, she could have as much as she wanted.

Kelly loaded her plate and sat down in the common area beside a wall of windows. Up and down and up and down. She couldn't escape it. The same magnificent ocean taunted her again.

"Looks like we're in for some rough seas today," a friendly old man chuckled. "Better not eat too much."

All she could do was groan.

"No patch, hey?" He tapped behind his ear.

Kelly shook her head, "Nope! I didn't get the memo." She poked at her plate and pushed it aside.

"I'm sorry, young lady."

He dragged his chair up to her table and made himself comfortable. "The wife made the same mistake you did when we first started cruising. Spent the whole week with her head in the toilet."

Lovely!

"No worries. You can always take a pill instead. It'll do the trick, too, except it makes you sleepy. Go see the ship's doctor."

Kelly thanked him for his thoughtful advice.

"Anyways... My name is Chester Mason," the jolly plump man extended his hand to shake hers. "Pleased to meet you!"

At least someone was talking to her.

"Kelly Preston," she answered. She shook his puffy hand as he held hers with both of his, holding it for a moment too long. *Wait, is he flirting or just being nice? It was hard to tell.*

Most of the time, Kelly couldn't tell the difference when men approached her like that, but this guy was old enough to be her grandfather. Maybe he was just being nice. He seemed like a sweet old man.

"Pleased to meet you, my dear? Are you travelling alone?"

"Um, *why?*"

"Oh, missy!" he chuckled, "I don't bite. It's just a friendly conversation. You looked like you needed a friend."

That was an understatement.

"Thank you," she started to warm up to him. "Your friendship is welcome. I'm travelling alone, and it's pretty hard to make friends."

"Well, I'll tell you a little secret. On these big ships, they aren't as intimidating as they seem. The wife and I have made quite a lot of friends on these cruises. You see, it's international waters, and so it's like we're all equal here. You meet people from all over the world. Just hang out with us and we'll show you the ropes, maybe even go on some excursions together."

"Excursions? What kind of excursions?"

Chester scooted up to her real close. *Too close.* But it was okay because the old man was growing on her. He smelled surprisingly clean, like baby powder and aftershave.

"So…I brought me the list. You see," he pulled out the paper, "the key is to get off the ship whenever you can. Not today because we have a full day at sea, but we'll be in Ketchikan soon. Come with us and we'll take you around town. It's a pretty little place. There's a lot to do and see. They even have tours you can go on."

Kelly observed the list, smiling at the old man as he explained all the different things to do. Finally, for the first time on this trip, she started to feel comfortable, like she belonged, like she wasn't invisible anymore.

"Well, you've given me a lot to think about. I might take you up on the offer."

"Look here," Chester pointed, "there's this duck boat adventure tour you can go on. It's a hoot. Me and the wife just love it. We've been on it before. Why don't you come?"

Then, out of nowhere, a large, smiley-faced woman suddenly stood beside him. She laughed and put her hand on his shoulder. "I see you're at it again! Never a dull moment with my Chester-Pester!"

Cute!

The woman had an outgoing, bubbly personality. Her

unique style made her look important. Her blouse was full of colourful shiny sequins, like she was ready to perform on stage. Her fingers were adorned with multiple gold and diamond rings on just about every finger.

When she stood next to Chester, they looked like a mismatched couple. He was in a plain white t-shirt barely covering his bulging belly. She was perfectly dressed with coiffed white hair like a well put-together woman. She liked them immediately. They felt warm and inviting. As odd as they looked together, they seemed to fit like a glove.

I'd give anything for that.

"Pleased to meet you," she extended a hand. "My name is Tweety."

Kelly got up to shake the woman's hand, but instead, the friendly woman pulled her into a warm bear hug, almost against her will.

Chester stood up as well and grabbed a chair for her. "I've been telling this young lady about the excursions. She's coming with us, you know."

Kelly smirked, "Well, I said I might!"

"Honey, if this old fart invited you, then you'd better come. He won't let up until you agree! How do you think I ended up with him?" she chuckled.

"That's my little Tweety-Bird!" he grinned. They both leaned together and kissed each other on the lips.

Adorable!

"How long have you guys been married?"

"Do you remember, Chester?"

Chester shrugged like he didn't care.

"Oh, you old fool!" She rolled her eyes and chuckled. "You never stop teasing me! He pretends he doesn't care, but really he does."

Chester winked, then suddenly looked serious and went quiet. He took his wife's hand in his as he cleared his throat. "Well, you know, it's fifty years on Wednesday. You thought I forgot, didn't you, Tweets?"

"I know you better than that, you goofball," she winked.

The two of them made a good couple even in their old age. Kelly couldn't believe two people could stay married that long. What baffled her the most was how affectionate they still were toward each other, even after fifty years.

Kelly loved meeting the Masons and all their camaraderie, but she was afraid her nausea was coming back. Sitting by the wall-length windows watching the ocean rise and fall again had proven too much. "I'm going to have to excuse myself. I really don't feel well."

"I told her to go see the ship's doctor. She's turning into *Toiletbowl-Tweety*," he giggled.

"*Chester!* I can't believe you said that!" She scolded him. "You know I don't like it when you call me that. It's *not* funny!"

The old man put his foot in his mouth this time, and that was her cue to leave. "Sorry, folks, it's time for me to go. What's your cell number, and I'll call you when I'm feeling better."

The two of them suddenly gave her a blank stare. "Oh, we don't have those things."

Kelly grinned through the nausea. *Of course you don't.* "Well, I'm sure we'll see each other again. I'm on the Promenade deck in cabin 225 if you're looking for me. That, or we can meet back here anytime."

"Sounds good," Tweety nodded. "We're leaving too. I need to go kick an old man's butt!"

Sighing, Chester rubbed his bald head and rolled his eyes. "Ya, and I gotta go take my pills!"

Me too, Chester, me too!

READY OR NOT

He was almost ready for the first group. Getting the bookings had been a real challenge. The bigger guiding businesses kept taking all the work. The only way he got the bookings he did was to reduce the price.

Boone knew he wouldn't stay in business for long if this kept up.

The other guiding businesses he competed against had investors. He did not. It was just him and the plane. When parts broke down, all he had was what remained of his inheritance, which wasn't much.

He'd have to work hard to get people to sign up. Already, he had spent a small fortune on advertising. *Second Chance Bear Guides.* At least he had a group of four booked tomorrow morning from The Legacy Cruise Line. He was a bit worried because it hadn't docked yet.

The first group consisted of a couple of dads and their teenage boys. Taking teenagers up there always proved to be a challenge, one way or the other. Usually, he liked taking middle-aged athletic types. They were the easiest to guide, but at this point, he couldn't really be picky. He needed the business.

The second group of four from The Sunshine Liner were supposed to dock after them, and that made him rest easy. If there was a problem, he made sure there was a big enough gap between the two groups that he could still take them both. He'd just have to move some things around.

Boone already purchased all the permits, so they'd better show up. He realized the second group had two elderly people. That, he didn't like either. He'd have to go easy on them. Again, he needed the business, so he was willing to take just about anyone.

With his luck, they'd all cancel and he'd go bankrupt. His father went through that several times. He remembered him begging the bank manager for a loan on numerous occasions. It was a hard thing to watch his father turn into a mooch.

Now I get it, Dad. It's a tough business. Still, his father made it way worse, like pouring salt on a wound. He ruined his own business and everyone's life in the process.

Boone witnessed the ups and downs firsthand. Things seemed to be a mess for a long time. Then, his mom moved out after he graduated from high school. She got a place of her own and said she couldn't take it anymore. *No doubt!*

His father's unpredictable drinking kept getting worse, like Dr. Jekyll and Mr. Hyde. One minute he was everyone's buddy, and the next minute he was angry and drunk. It was about time his mother stood up for herself. He was proud of her.

Being a spouse of an alcoholic was very difficult; she would always tell him. He understood. Being a child of one was no better.

After she left him, his mother started a great Tlingit artisan gift shop in Angoon with her sister. She displayed her art, as well as sourced art on consignment. It was very profitable. Then she got sick and had to sell everything she had worked so hard for.

Why did life have to be so tough?

It seemed unstable most of the time. Especially right now, starting a new guiding business. Every part of it had been a challenge. From the headache of trying to renew his pilot's license after his incarceration, to getting a business license. He couldn't forget the ridiculous amount of money he was forced to spend on insurance.

That was just insane!

But...life was a gamble. *Scratch that.* The old Boone would have said that. What he really meant was that God had a way of putting you through something over and over again until you learn what He's trying to teach you.

"Discipline," the pastor would say, "that's how you know

you're His."

Some lessons were painful. At times, it seemed as though God was very far away. Things happened in prison that he couldn't even speak about, yet God was there in the quiet.

He found Jesus that first year while praying with Pastor Tom, but God didn't take him out of the fire immediately. He protected him while he was still there. All those times it could've gone the wrong way, but it didn't.

God's grace was kind and merciful.

It could have been him with the extended sentence. Yet, there he was, an entrepreneur. Granted, not an official AME like he wanted...but that was okay with him. Right now, it was more about therapy than anything else. There were a lot of things he had to work through.

Mostly, he had to heal.

The ocean slopped against the twin pontoons as the cool sea breeze picked up. It was getting late, and the weather was turning. It was something that happened a lot in Alaska. One minute it was sunny, and the next it was rainy. In fact, it was rainy almost all the time. Hardly therapeutic for sun seekers, that's for sure!

Unfortunately, that wasn't Boone.

He didn't inherit his mother's lovely brown skin. Nope. Give him some sunscreen, shade, and a pair of sunglasses, and he was good to go. No sun for him. Gingers weren't made for that. All he ever got was a burn and freckles.

Alaska must have been made for the Scottish.

There were so many things he loved about this place, like the mountains and the wildlife, but the smell had to be Boone's favourite. There was nothing like it in the entire world. The ocean air had a way of soothing the soul.

Except for tonight.

Tonight, a storm was brewing, and that worried him. Bitter winds began to whip across his red, bearded face. He secured the fully stocked plane, and that's all he could do. Hopefully, it would be there in the morning, safe and sound. His business depended upon it.

Now, to get back to his house. It was a short walk up the hill to the small, modest rental he called home for the past year. His neighbour would be worried. She was like a mother to him, always coming over with a meal.

Boone hoped she had something waiting for him tonight.

Hard to believe he spent the entire day down on the Juneau seaplane dock. He got all the final prep done, including the last bit of engine work. If not for the hired help, he never would have gotten it all done.

This is it! Ready or not!

THE SETUP

Kelly realized Chester and Tweety had mobility issues that required some help. Working in home care for a few years now has given her insight into the old couple's situation. Chester with his bad knees and Tweety with her swollen ankles. It was hard to believe they didn't use canes.

"Honestly! I can get you both some canes," she said. "It's no trouble."

Chester huffed and puffed as he took Tweety's arm. "The day I use a cane is the day they put me in the grave," he fussed.

"He's so stubborn," Tweety said, "but I'm no better, I guess. Maybe we should let her help, dear. Our ailments are much worse today. We're probably not used to all this walking."

"No, it's all the sitting," he replied. "On the plane. On the ship. Cramps me up. Remember the last cruise? It took a few days for us to limber up, then we were just fine."

"That was years ago, Chester! We ain't spring chickens anymore!"

Kelly stood there with her hands on her hips, listening to them both arguing and making excuses. It was a simple fix. She wasn't taking no for an answer. There was no way she was going anywhere with these two like this. What if one of them fell and broke a hip? What if there was an injury that landed them in the hospital?

Nope! She wouldn't take no for an answer.

"You guys, stop!" she said. "Why don't you sit down on this bench, and I'll be right back!"

In a hurry, Kelly arranged to get some canes for her two elderly companions. All she had to do was talk to the ship's doctor. It was that simple. They made a big deal about nothing.

Within fifteen minutes, she came back with canes in hand. Chester and Tweety were still sitting on the bench where she had left them. She couldn't believe they'd come all this way without them.

"I ain't using that!" Chester leaned against his wife. "I'll look like an old fool."

"You *are* an old fool," Tweety laughed.

"Thanks a lot!" Chester pouted, refusing to budge.

"I'm sorry, but if I have to use one, so do you!"

Kelly chuckled under her breath. They were both comical. All she knew was she had to get this old guy to understand it was necessary. He could barely walk. She decided to use a tactic from her job.

The straightforward approach.

"Look, Chester," she told him, "For the last couple of days, I've seen how much your knee bothers you. I should have insisted while we were on the ship, but you are much worse today, and you know it. *Use the cane!*"

Tweety nodded her head as if to say thank you. Kelly could tell it took the burden off of her, literally. He would stop leaning on her then.

They both took the canes and stood up.

"I guess it's not that bad," Chester grinned, "but where is yours, little lady? You need to match us."

"Funny!" Kelly was growing comfortable with them. She was glad she found some travelling companions. It sure beat loneliness!

"So, what's on the agenda here, folks?" Kelly asked as she stood with them on the Ketchikan dock. The place was peaceful and quaint, straight out of a fairytale. Its colourful houses nestled into the side of a hill, lining a picturesque harbour loaded with sailboats on every dock.

Tweety looked at her watch. "Well," she said, "we still have a few minutes before Parker gets here."

"Who?"

"Our grandson," Tweety replied matter-of-factly, "he

booked everything through the why-five. We don't know how to do that. Chester told him what he wanted, and Parker did all the planning. He couldn't join us until now. He's a busy lawyer, you know, but you'll be perfect for him."

Perfect for him?

"Oh!" Kelly was taken aback. Had she known their grandson was coming along, she might not have agreed to come. Being a third wheel was not her style, or, whatever this was.

"Maybe I should let you guys go do whatever you have planned," Kelly told them. "I don't want to be a bother."

"A bother?" Tweety said. "Honey, you are not a bother. You are just what the doctor ordered! Why would you think you're a bother?"

"I-I didn't expect this, that's all. I thought you guys were on this cruise alone. I feel so stupid."

"Oh, honey!"

Kelly thought maybe she could just escape into the crowd somehow, but they would notice. They would think she was rude for ditching them. But who was this lawyer? And why did they think she was perfect? Why didn't they mention him earlier? The last thing she needed was this.

She didn't feel comfortable coming along now. Nor did she feel like meeting their grandson, even if he was an important lawyer. That made her cringe even more.

"I just remembered; I have to go back to the ship."

"What for, dear?" Tweety asked.

"I-um, I don't feel very well."

That was the truth. She didn't feel well, not now. Not with their grandson coming. Kelly felt her stomach churn. Why was she so upset? It's not like she hadn't talked to total strangers before. She visited with a professor at the airport and others along the way. She was getting better at meeting people.

So, why was she so apprehensive about meeting this grandson of theirs? What was it about him that made her nervous?

"Nonsense!" Tweety grinned, "You're just fine. We think the

two of you will get along like two peas in a pod. You're a perfect match."

And there it was.

The reason she felt so awkward was that they seemed to spring this on her for a reason. They could have mentioned it earlier, but they didn't. They didn't for a reason. It was a setup.

"Look," she said, "I know what you're doing. I-I don't feel comfortable with this. I just came out of a relationship. I'm not going to be good company."

In other words, she didn't want to be set up with their grandson, even if he was a big-shot lawyer or a so-called perfect match. She wasn't ready for that.

"It will be fine. He's really nice."

"No-um, I'm going back to the ship."

Chester suddenly grabbed Kelly's hand and squeezed it. He had a calming effect on her. He was a kind old man, and she felt terrible acting like this. Maybe she shouldn't be so skittish.

Remember, Kelly, you were going to bloom? Maybe she should take her advice and give the guy a chance.

"Come on," Chester smiled. "I promise you'll have a good time. Besides, we will probably need a fourth person. I see Parker now."

"Okay then," Kelly bit her lip, hoping she wasn't going to regret it, "let's go meet your grandson."

If she didn't know any better, she'd say this was the plan all along.

I CAN PAY

Parker was bad news. She knew that right from the start. The moment she met him, Kelly knew he was a womanizer. Sure, he was tall, dark, and handsome, but she tried not to notice. The old Kelly would have been interested, but not anymore. She made a vow to stay away from guys like him.

Always attracted to the wrong man.

At first, she had to do a double-take. He didn't look anything like his short, apple-shaped grandparents. But then, that was the inevitable. Growing old was not kind to the body.

Kelly hoped she wouldn't turn into the old people she worked with in the nursing home. They sat like zombies in their chairs most of the time. That was not happening to her!

For a moment, Kelly allowed her mind to drift. It was a lot better than listening to Parker brag about himself. They just finished the duck tour and had coffee at a seaside restaurant overlooking the Ketchikan harbour.

Perhaps, she was jaded. She'd seen his type before, even dated them. Always bad news. Yet, at the start, they seemed normal. Then the charisma slowly turned into narcissism. By then, it was usually too late. She was too far into the relationship to get out easily. *This was not happening again!*

He was definitely not a perfect match!

"Hello?" Tweety touched her arm. "You look a million miles away, dear. What's wrong?"

"Nothing. I guess I'm just tired."

Why did she have to lie? She really wanted to say she regretted coming along. She regretted letting them set her up with their grandson. This wasn't working.

"It was fun, wasn't it?" Chester beamed.

Kelly nodded and forced a smile to appease the old man. "Yes, it was, but I think it's time to head back to the ship." She looked at her smartwatch. "We don't want them to leave without us."

"Well, before we do," Parker winked at her, "I just want to go over the itinerary. I've booked something amazing for you, Grandad." He pretended to wipe a tear from his cheek, sniffed and paused like he was choking back emotions. Then he looked at her for cause and effect. *What was this guy trying to pull?*

She didn't trust him one bit.

He was not the kind of person to tear up. He was a lawyer, for heaven's sake. He was also a con man and knew how to play the room. Kelly could tell he was quite good at that. He seemed to be over-emotional for some reason, and that alarmed her. She'd seen it all before.

Something else was going on here, but she couldn't put her finger on it. He acted like Ted with the emotional tricks. He had an agenda. Typically, a narcissist is incapable of doing things selflessly. I'm sure this itinerary was all about him.

"And what about your grandmother?" Kelly asked point-blank.

"Excuse me?"

"You said you booked it for your *grandad*," Kelly analyzed. "Your grandmother is here too. Don't you think you should include her? Why is it all about Chester?"

Parker's fake smile waned, and he bit back hard. "Darling, if I wanted your opinion, I would have asked for it. Now, keep your mouth shut! You have no idea what's going on here."

Try me!

"PARKER!"

The man glared at his grandmother with eyes of steel. He controlled his grandfather, too. "This trip is for you, buddy," he leaned in and grabbed his arm. "Remember? You told me you wanted it this way."

Tweety was fuming. "I'm sorry, Kelly. Parker forgets to use

his manners," she scolded, then shook her head and turned away.

"Anyhoo..," Parker continued like nothing happened.

Kelly was not having it. There was no way she was letting this go. He was manipulating these sweet people. "I thought this was for their 50th anniversary."

Then Chester interrupted. "My dear," he sighed, "you don't understand, Parker is trying to..."

"Stop it!" Tweety interrupted before he could finish his sentence. "Can we just hear what Parker has planned, first? I asked him to go the extra mile. I asked him to get four tickets just in case Sara changed her mind."

Now Kelly was confused. "Sara?"

"*Grandma*, I told you it was an absolute no! I got her a ticket for nothing!" And you," Parker directed his anger at Kelly, "who are you anyway? Why are you even here? JUST LEAVE!"

Immediately, Kelly stood up and grabbed her purse. She was not staying where she wasn't welcome. She knew it was a mistake hanging out with them. These people were hiding something. Their narcissistic grandson was playing them for some reason, and she knew it. He probably wanted his inheritance.

Chester began to cry.

"Now look what you did, you stupid..."

"Enough!" Tweety scolded her grandson. "You do not speak to her like that. She is not Sara! You blew it with her, and now you're blowing it with this nice young girl, too. We thought the two of you would hit it off. That's why we invited her! Now... Kelly, sit down!"

"I don't need you matching me up, Grandma. Look what happened the last time."

"That was your fault, young man!"

"FINE! Can we just get on with it, then?"

Chester continued to cry.

"Look what you are doing to him. He doesn't need this right now. He can't cope with you and everything else that's going on with him."

Again, Chester sobbed. *Can the man not speak for himself?*

What on earth is going on here? Kelly pursed her lips and sat quietly. Against her better judgment, she was going to see how this panned out. Until now, Chester and Tweety have only shown their sweet side to her. This was something else. Something she couldn't put her finger on.

"Now, stop being so rude and tell us what you were able to book!" the stern woman commanded her grandson. "Hopefully it's what he asked for."

Parker glared at Kelly for a moment, as if it were her fault. "Fine! Grandad..," he took a breath, "I was able to book the tour you wanted."

Chester looked stunned. "*Bears?* he cupped his hands together, "I'm finally going to see my bears?"

"That's right, grandpa!"

Chester began to sob again. If Kelly didn't know any better, she'd say the trip meant more to him than he let on. She'd seen it before, working in the nursing home. Family members grant their loved ones one last wish. *Was he dying?*

Kelly kept quiet and let him continue. If Chester was terminally ill, he didn't look like it. Sure, he had bad knees and an oversized belly, but he didn't look like he was about to die. *Some don't, maybe.* If her assumptions were correct, she wasn't going to ask to confirm it.

"So, I booked a fly-in bear tour to a place called The Fortress of the Bear. It's on Admiralty Island just outside of Juneau."

"You booked it for four, right?" Tweety asked.

Yes, Grandmother, I told you I invited Sara, but she wouldn't come. We've been over this. The ticket is non-refundable and a total waste of money, but YOU wanted it."

"Then, Kelly is going in Sara's place. Aren't you dear?"

"I-um..," Kelly didn't know if she dared say no to the woman.

"Gran, it doesn't work like that! She's NOT coming!"

"Yes, she is!"

"Fine, but don't blame me if it doesn't work out."

What a jerk! She should go just to tick him off. "I can pay!" Kelly shot her mouth off before thinking.

"Then it's settled!" Tweety banged her cane on the ground. "We're ALL going! Chester, you got your dying wish!"

THE DATE

That night, Chester had insisted Parker take Kelly out to dinner to make amends. They settled on a high-end restaurant situated at the front of the ship with a clear view of the ocean.

"Look," Kelly said, "I just agreed to this charade to appease your grandfather. "I told him it was a bad idea. You're not even my type."

"I can assure you; the feeling is mutual."

The man couldn't even be a gentleman. What kind of guy says that on a date, or even a non-date like this? The least he could do was be civil.

"Let's just order and get this over with. I can't even stand to look at you," she turned her head toward the window.

"You know, I've dated a lot of women, and I can usually tell. Secretly, you think I'm hot. Don't deny it!"

Kelly wanted to slap him. He was so arrogant and full of himself. It didn't matter that he was dressed in a suit and tie that made him look like he was a GQ model. No matter how debonair he looked, she was not interested. This man was off limits.

"What kind of a line is that?"

"You like it?"

"NO!" Kelly flipped her long blonde hair over her shoulder and looked at the sea rising and falling. The two of them sat in an awkward silence until the waiter came over to take their order.

"The lady will have the Veal Cordon Bleu, and I'll have the Filet Mignon, medium rare, please. And bring us a bottle of your best Chardonnay."

The waiter bowed as Parker handed him two one-hundred-dollar bills. "Thank you, sir." Then he headed for the kitchen with a smile.

"Gratuities, you know. I can afford it."

"I can't believe you," she whispered, trying to keep her voice down, "you throw your money around like it's nothing. You don't even ask me what I want. You just assume. You don't know me, you arrogant jerk!"

Why should she even stay? The guy was obnoxious. She didn't owe him anything, or anyone else for that matter. It was time to get out of there. Kelly could hear the little voice in her head reminding her of the repeated pattern. *You always run from difficult things! Stay!*

Against her better judgment, Kelly tried to breathe. She cooled down and gave the guy a chance to defend himself.

"Darling," he said, "I know girls like you. You pretend to hate me, though you really don't. You can't even make up your mind what you want to wear, let alone what you want to eat. How many outfits did you try on before you settled on that thing you're wearing? It's ugly! Where'd you get it, the thrift store?"

That's it! No more chances!

Kelly slapped her napkin down on the table. What an insult! She was not going through with this now! The man was ignorant! She stood up and tugged at her indigenous dress she purchased at the Trading Post in Ketchikan.

"Firstly, *you jerk!* I happen to like what I have on. Secondly, I know what I want to eat. If you bothered to ask me, like most gentlemen do, I need a gluten-free meal. I have Celiac Disease. Not that you even know what that means."

"Oh, it figures. You're one of *those!*"

Kelly burned with anger. She pushed her chair away and grabbed her purse. "I'm leaving!"

"You can't! My grandfather is expecting us to make up. You don't want to disappoint him; he's a dying man. What am I supposed to tell him now?"

"I don't know, lie to him like you always do."

"Ooo, sassy!" Parker grinned, "*I like that!*"

Just then, a different waiter came to the table with French

bread in hand. He cleared his throat. "Madam? Is everything okay?"

"No, it's not okay!" She felt her face flush. "I can't eat that! I can't eat Veal Cordon Bleu! It's breaded!" she glared at Parker. "And I..."

Breathe!

Dizziness hit her suddenly, and the room started spinning. She gulped hard, feeling a sense of doom. Nausea churned her stomach, as bile rose in her throat. *Was it a panic attack?*

Maybe she was seasick.

"Madam, are you okay?"

Parker stood up and laughed. "She tends to drink too much," he told the waiter and everyone else that was watching. "I'll take my drunk date back to her room, I guess. Nothing to see here, folks."

What?

How dare he? She doesn't even drink. She can't because most alcoholic beverages are made with grains, which she can't have. He had no right to tell people she was drunk when she wasn't.

Kelly grabbed her head and tried to steady herself. Sweat ran down her forehead, triggering another bout of vertigo. She held the back of the chair for support, but it wasn't helping.

Everything was spinning out of control.

She tried to breathe. It was the worst feeling she'd ever experienced. Nothing would stop the spinning. All she could do was hold on for dear life as her eyes seemed to involuntarily jump from side to side. *What was this?*

"I-I need help!"

The waiters stood watching. Everyone stood watching, but nobody seemed to be helping her. They all looked at Parker.

He didn't seem to care. Maybe he thought she was faking it. Maybe they all thought she was faking it. Or, maybe they really did think she was drunk.

The spinning suddenly stopped, hopefully for good. She looked around the restaurant, and everyone was staring. How embarrassing!

"I-I need to go," she grabbed her purse, attempting to walk, but she dropped it, and had to bend down to get it.

"You should have seen your face," Parker laughed, making fun of her. "This has got to be a first."

But Kelly felt it come on again. It was the bending down that triggered it. Round and round the room spun. She couldn't hold her balance this time. She teetered back and forth, nearly collapsing.

Parker grabbed her elbow this time. "Must you keep doing this?" he whispered, "You're making a spectacle out of me."

Out of *him*? Rage filled her as she ripped her elbow free. "Don't you touch me, you selfish jerk!"

Suddenly, vomit rose quickly in her throat, and she puked all over Parker's expensive suit. Everyone around them gasped.

"Oh gross! Now look what you did!" Parker gave her heck, acting all embarrassed. He observed his vomit-stained suit and shook his head. "I told you not to drink so much!"

Kelly was furious, but she couldn't do anything about him at the moment. The room kept spinning round and round. She had no choice but to lean on him, but he pushed her away.

This time, she started to see stars. This time, it felt different. A woozy feeling came over her as she felt her legs give way.

The last thing she heard was, *"Grab her!"*

FIRST GROUP

After a very rewarding trip with the first group, Boone was pleased that everyone gave him a five-star review.

It was exhausting doing everything himself, but very lucrative. He hoped it would be enough to keep the business afloat.

Thankfully, he was able to hire the high-school boys again. He needed the extra manpower to help unload the plane and clean it out. With tourists, you never knew what to expect. Some were fine, but others left garbage everywhere.

At least he'd have a day to recuperate before the next group arrived.

"I know, it's terrible!" Boone told the boys, "Just do the best you can." The plane resembled a high-school locker room, and it smelled like it, too. Someone had very bad B.O., and the teenagers left gum on the floor and candy wrappers everywhere. One of them even puked on the floor.

Terrible was an understatement.

Boone hoped the next group had manners, and everyone showered before boarding. Five hours with a small group is a long time in rank conditions.

The bears didn't behave either, which was a bit odd. They should be preoccupied with the mating season in full swing, but the group of bears they watched seemed to come too close for his liking.

Though he knew the ins and outs of bear watching, he still felt uneasy with their odd movements. Perhaps it was the boys' bad B.O. that made them aggressive. Or, more likely, it was their incessant fooling around. He didn't know how many times he had to tell them to settle down and stop throwing rocks at the bears. That was an absolute no-no.

In fact, Boone had to take the adults aside and let them know the trip would end if the boys didn't stop. All he needed was an incident. Heaven forbid, an injury or a casualty happened on his watch. They would shut down the Tongass National Forest. That meant no more tours for the foreseeable future.

Thankfully, that didn't happen.

In the future, Boone made a mental note to make sure the rules were understood before bringing a group into one of the most dangerous parts of Alaska. If, for any reason, he felt his group was in danger, he'd be sure to pull them out before an incident occurred.

Thankfully, nothing bad happened, and he could stop stressing about the what-ifs. God had his back anyway. He always did. Though these boys tested him, they made it through unharmed.

People don't realize the full scope of the business. It's not just about packing them in and packing them out. It's about keeping them safe. He's responsible for every single person he guides in. That's a huge responsibility, and one he doesn't take lightly.

Unlike his father, he took many courses to do what he does. Most of them were taken when his father was still alive. All he had to do when he got out of prison was update some of his certifications. At least he cared enough to make sure he knew what he was doing.

"We're done, boss," the boys told him. They stood there on the dock with a smelly bucket and mop in tow. One of them had a mask on still.

"Oh, *c'mon,* it wasn't that bad, was it?"

"Yes! It was!"

"You need to pay us double for that gross mess!"

Boone figured the boys were right. He pulled out some cash and paid them twice as much as he intended. That's the cost of doing business. He valued the boys' help and he wanted to keep them as employees, if you could call them that.

Either way, he was thankful for the help. As they left the dock and drove off in their car, he locked things up and headed up the hill. Maybe his neighbour had a meal waiting again.

He was much too tired to cook.

"Evening, Mary!" Boone greeted his landlady as he approached his cozy red and white rental nestled up against hers. She was a small, round Mennonite woman with a traditional scarf on her head. No matter what the weather, she always wore a dress and stockings.

"Kind of cold out," he smiled. "You need to put a coat on, my dear!"

"Good'n Owen's, Mien Jung," she greeted him in her low German dialect. Translated, it meant good evening, my boy. Boone was catching on fast thanks to Google.

She didn't always speak German, but every now and then she tested him with it. He was used to her broken English. Kind of a cross between both languages. It brought character to her jolly old soul. He was glad God found him such a friendly landlady.

Her customs were different, but that was okay with Boone. The two of them got along great, and that was all that mattered."

"I brought you supper."

"Dat is groot."

"No, no, Mien Jung," she teased. "You would say, dat is fein! Groot means...how you say?" Mary wrestled with the word. "Big! Meal no groot. Meal is fein!"

Boone laughed. As good as he thought he was at Plattdeutsch, he still had a lot to learn. "Well, Mary, either way, I'm grateful for the meal."

She handed him a steaming plate of perogies and farmer sausage smothered with roasted onions and sour cream. His absolute favourite! It was her special recipe. The one she said was made just for him. She had no idea how much something like this meant to him after the kind of day he had.

"Dankscheen!"

The old woman smiled and bowed several times as her dress fluttered in the wind. She was cold, but she wouldn't go inside. He hoped she didn't intend for him to eat it outside.

"You'd better go inside, Mary! The wind is picking up!"

Mary shivered as she hugged her shaking body. Her eyes started to tear up, and Boone wondered if she was just glad to see him or if something was wrong. "Are you okay?"

"Ich bin okay," she sniffled, "but this...soddbrennen," she said, grabbing her chest. "How you say, hoat?"

Boone would have to look those words up. She didn't seem like herself, but then he was tired. Everything looked and sounded odd to him right now. As long as she said she was okay, that's all that mattered.

She shook her head again. "Ich bin okay, Mien Jung," she patted his back and turned around to go inside.

Boone grabbed his hot meal and headed for the door. Before he opened it, he turned around one more time. "Mary, again, thank you so much for the supper. It means a lot to me. If you need anything at all, please let me know. Anything!"

She nodded and went inside.

BANG BANG BANG

It was a little after 10 p.m., and the sun had finally set over Juneau, Alaska. As Boone peeked out his kitchen window, he could see that Mary still had her lights on. *That's odd.* She was usually early to bed and early to rise, and was known to keep a strict schedule.

The kitchen faucet ran as he rinsed his plate and set it on the dish rack to dry. He stood there for a moment, watching her window. If he were able to see her, he'd relax a little. Or else, he'd have to give her a call. Really, it was none of his business why she was up so late. It's not like they kept track of each other. Yet, she told him she always watched for his plane to come in.

Boone realized he meant more to the old woman than he realized. *Oh, Mary, you mean a lot to me too!*

Then, a shadow crossed the closed living room sheers. She *was* up! Boone's gut told him something was wrong. She was pacing back and forth. Maybe she was having an intense conversation on the phone. Who would be calling at this hour? She told him she didn't have any living relatives. But the landline was in the kitchen, not there. She didn't have a cell phone either. *Ah, but she did have a portable phone.* That must be it!

Still, Boone figured he'd better give her a call just in case.

Busy!

So, she *was* on the phone. That put Boone's mind at ease. It wasn't polite to be nosy anyway. He turned off the kitchen light and headed for the bedroom. Sleep couldn't come fast enough. It had been a long, gruelling day and he was beat. He pulled open the covers and wrapped himself tight. The wind was still howling outside, and that meant the plane was knocking around. Thankfully, it was secured pretty good. He shouldn't have to worry about any kind of damage. It could stay there until the next tour. All he had to do was stock it later tomorrow.

The old-fashioned lamp on the nightstand beamed in Boone's eyes. The thing must have been from the 70s. He pulled the dangling chain to turn it off and welcomed the dark. It was time to sleep.

Prayers first! Yes, he couldn't forget that. *"Thank you, Lord, for this adventurous day. But can you please let the next group be more mature? Amen!"* He punched his pillow until he got it just right. Then, buzzing on the nightstand beside him, the bedtime reminder went off on his phone. He forgot to silence it.

As Boone reached over to grab it, something gnawed at him. He forgot to look up Mary's new words. It would just take a moment. He pulled the lamp chain again, illuminating the room. Now what was that word again? One long word, and one short one. What was it? Hoot? Hoap? No, it was hoat.

Boone looked up the short word first. It meant *Heart.* Was she telling him she loved him? Then he moved to the long word. It sounded like someone's name. Brendan or something like that. Except, it had a word before it. Sud-brendan maybe. No, it was Soddbrennan. He looked that one up too and was a bit startled to find out it meant *heartburn.* What? Was Mary telling him he'd get heartburn from her meal? Why would she? It definitely didn't give him heartburn. It was an amazing meal!

Boone sat straight up in bed and put the pieces together. Mary patted her chest. She said, heart. She said, Heartburn. Suddenly, he bolted out of bed, took his phone with him, and ran to the kitchen window. Her light was still on. Panic struck him. He threw a jacket on and slid his bare feet into his boots.

Like lightning he bolted to her front door, banging, hoping he was wrong. "Mary! Mary!" he pounded. No answer. He went around back and tried that door. *Bang bang bang!* Still no answer. He tried the doorknob. Locked. Then he started dialling her number. Still busy. *Bang bang bang!*

Luckily, he knew where she hid the spare key.

"Mary, are you okay?" he yelled as he unlocked the door.

"Mary! Mary!"

As Boone entered the living room, there she was, crumpled over in her recliner, holding her chest. She was still conscious, but started to cry. "I know, dear. We'll get you help." He immediately called 911 and got a dispatcher on the line. They were sending an ambulance to get her. They helped him assess her and made sure he stayed on the phone until help arrived.

"Possible heart attack," he told the EMTs as they entered Mary's house. They asked him to step aside so they could work on her. They were the professionals. Boone was glad for that. Though he was fully trained in first aid and CPR, he was thankful to pass the torch to someone else. How could he miss the warning signs? He should have picked up on them instead of being so self-absorbed.

"Are you next of kin?"

"Ummm!" Boone looked at Mary.

"Yes!" Mary nodded, "he's... *Mien Jung!*"

Boone knelt beside her and held her hand. "That's German for, *I'm her boy.*"

"Okay, then, follow us," the EMT told him, "We're taking her to Bartlett Regional Hospital, and it looks like she wants you there."

Boone held her hand and reassured her that he would be right behind them. The woman teared up and nodded her head. He knew she needed him. She had nobody else. He ran to his house, grabbed a change of clothes, his wallet, and keys to his old beater parked out front. He rarely drove it and hoped it still fired up. Either way, he was going to be there for Mary, even if he had to call a cab.

One thing was for sure: he wasn't getting any sleep tonight.

FOOD COMA

Twenty hours had passed since they brought Mary to the hospital.

She seemed to be doing a lot better, but not out of the woods yet. They were still waiting on a few more tests. From what the doctor confirmed so far, there was no indication of a heart attack or stroke. That was a relief. Instead, they thought it might be her gallbladder.

"Go home, *Mien Jung!*" Mary patted Boone's tattooed arm. "You need sleep!"

Boone looked at his watch and sighed. Yes, that was correct. He hadn't slept at all last night and only caught a few winks during the day in between tests. He didn't want to leave her until the last few test results came back. He'd never forgive himself if something happened to her after he left.

Right now, he had to lighten the mood. If Mary were worried about him, that would prolong her recovery time. Laughter was good medicine; his aunt would tell him. That's what Mary needed. Now, what were those words he Googled this morning?

"*Ja!* I can sleep *wen ik dood!*" Boone grinned. He had been practicing. There was nothing else to do but study Plattdeutsch.

"WEN IK DOOD?" Mary burst into laughter. Then, winced in pain.

Maybe it wasn't such a good idea to make her laugh right now. "Mary! I'm sorry. I couldn't resist. Are you okay?"

"Ja!"

It was kind of funny, though. Boone could tell Mary enjoyed it even though it brought her pain. The old woman was a tough bird. He could tell she was used to dismissing her own problems.

From the stories she told him all day, it was no wonder. The woman had quite a history.

"If you no sleep, you will *dood!* Yes?"

Boone chuckled. "Yes, Mary! I get it!"

He looked at his watch again, realizing the test results would likely not be in today. "I'll head home!"

Hopefully, he could swing by tomorrow morning before his next tour. The Sunshine Liner would likely be late anyway, due to bad weather last night. The seas were pretty choppy. Thankfully, the forecast was for clear blue skies all day today. Tomorrow was supposed to be the same. Perfect weather for flying and guiding.

If it hadn't been for his teenage employees stocking the plane for him this afternoon, he would've had to leave Mary. He'll have to remember to give them both a good bonus. Hopefully, they packed everything he texted them. For a bear guide as complex as his, it was crucial to have all the safety gear and just-in-case items on every flight.

He made a mental note to double-check the gear.

"Mien Jung?" Mary called out to him as he put his jacket on.

"Ja?"

"You get key. Perogies in fridge. Ja?" she nodded.

He knew what she meant, and he was not turning *that* down! "Thank you, Mary!"

Once he knew she was okay, Boone kissed her on the forehead. He looked around the hospital room, hoping she'd be safe while he was gone.

Anything could happen. She was an old woman. Memories of his mother flooded back. It was this very hospital she died in. By the time they flew her from Angoon to Juneau, she didn't have much time left.

She wanted to spend her last days in Angoon. There was nothing more they could do for her anyway. That's what she always told him. She'd tried everything. Chemo. Radiation. None of it worked.

All it did was turn her into a shell of herself. It took her youthful glow. It took her energy. It took her hair. All she could do was wrap her bald head in colourful scarves, much like Mary's scarf.

The memory burned.

He remembered the last time he left the hospital before his mom died. It was a sunny day, much like today. "Go home," she told him. "Get some rest," she said. Much like Mary told him.

No harm in that, right?

Except when it's the last time you'll ever see your loved one again. Boone's heart ached. He reeled over his decision to leave that day. He never got to say goodbye. Not really.

Sure, he spent endless days by her side, but that's not the same. He never got to hold her hand and say goodbye. He knew he'd meet her again in heaven. Thank the Lord for that.

She was a believer way before he found Jesus. He never knew. She kept it to herself. He was told she met a tourist who led her to Christ. He bought her art. That was the story, anyway.

Oh, how he missed her.

Lord, I don't want these emotions. It's this hospital. He had to get out of there. Boone realized hospitals were not his favourite place to be, especially this one.

Did good things even come from there? He couldn't answer that; all he knew was the sooner he made it through the door, the better.

Take care of her, Jesus.

Boone headed to his old beater in the parking lot and roared it to life. He made a beeline for Mary's place as quickly as he could, glad to be out of that hospital.

First things first. His stomach.

By the time Boone scarfed down another one of Mary's special meals, he was absolutely beat! His eyelids were heavy, and it was finally time to sleep. First, he had to go home.

Once he cleaned Mary's dish and tidied up, he shut off her lights and headed across the driveway. As he laboured up the stairs to his kitchen, he realized he had over-stuffed himself.

Oh boy! His belly was paying for it now.

Unbuckling his belt, Boone decided not to go to the dock tonight. He'd check the gear in the morning. He was much too tired and full. Surely the boys got it all stocked anyway. He had to trust his employees at some point. He didn't even care that he couldn't find his phone. It could all wait until morning.

He dragged his tired, over-stuffed belly to his bedside, flung open the covers, and collapsed into a food coma.

Sleep!

THE GASLIGHTING

After her fainting spell, Kelly found herself in her room, covered up in bed from head to toe. She peeked under the blankets, and all she had on was her underwear.

What on earth?

Looking around her small stateroom, blurry-eyed and groggy, she saw the doctor, Tweety, and that-that man. *Parker!* It was all his fault.

"Why are you guys here?" she whispered, half-conscious.

What she really wanted to say was, *Get out! Get out of my room, now!* But, of course. She had to be a people pleaser, and that was hard for her to say.

Heaven forbid she should hurt someone else's feelings.

Even if someone was gaslighting her, she rarely had the nerve to stand up for herself. Most of the time, she couldn't even recognize the abuse. Though tonight in the restaurant with *him*, she did. It was one of the rare occasions.

Good job, girl!

Kelly wiped her sweaty forehead and cleared her throat. How could they not hear her the first time?

They carried on in the corner louder than a bunch of magpies. They were too focused on their own talking to pay attention to her.

"*A-hem!*" She cleared her throat and tried again.

The group suddenly turned.

"Well, look who's awake," Parker grinned. "Sleeping Beauty is alive, and I didn't even have to kiss her."

Oh please! Not on your life, buddy!

"What's going on?"

Tweety put her arm on her grandson and answered. "Well,

it appears you had a fainting spell, my dear. How do you feel?"

"Woozy. Where are my clothes?"

"Oh, Babe, I'm not that kind of guy," Parker teased.

Why was he being so weird?

Tweety gave him a look. "Stop!"

Kelly felt a panic attack coming on. Tears welled in her eyes. This was embarrassing and humiliating. Tweety was lovely, but her grandson had all the attributes of her former boyfriend, Ted. He was clearly a gaslighting narcissist.

"Miss Preston, it appears you are seasick," the doctor told her. "But your boyfriend says you drank too much. That will only make matters worse."

Kelly's eyes narrowed. Anger burst through her mouth before she could stop herself. "NO! He is NOT my boyfriend! And NO, I wasn't drinking!"

"They all say that!" Parker chuckled at the doctor. "I've seen my share of inebriated clients, and this little lady is completely wasted!"

"I AM NOT!"

Tweety went to her bedside and sat down. She tried to comfort her and whispered in her ear. "My dear, I know my grandson is a lot, but try not to let him get under your skin. I'll kick him out if you want."

Kelly shook her head. "Yes, *please!*"

"Okay, Parker!" Tweety ordered, "Get out!"

There was no mincing words with Tweety. Kelly wished she were more like her. She always admired the tell-it-like-it-is types. Nothing seemed to faze them.

"Fine! I guess that's what I get for taking a girl on a date."

The man was ridiculous!

"Enough!" Tweety barked. "Do not badger the poor girl! She just needs to rest. Now, get out!"

"I said, Fine! Just remember," Parker smirked, "I didn't get her drunk, grandmother. She did that all on her own. She probably knocked back a bottle of Vodka before she met up with me. Don't blame me if she can't go on the bear tour tomorrow morning."

Unbelievable! The man was working the room. Typical lawyer! Or, should I say narc?

Before Kelly realized it, she opened her mouth and flipped a comeback. "Oh, I *fully* intend on being there!" Perhaps Tweety was rubbing off on her after all.

Before anyone could stop the lawyer's rebuttal, he cross-examined her like a pro. "Darling," he replied, "If your drinking gets in the way of my grandfather's dying wish, I will personally sue you for everything you've got. Are we clear?"

"Parker!" Tweety scolded him again, "Enough!"

The doctor hurried as he fumbled to grab his things. "I'll leave you folks to...*whatever is going on here.* Miss," he directed his gaze at Kelly, "let me know if you need anything else. I can order a special meal for you if you like. Tea and toast perhaps. Just let me know."

"Oh boy!" Parker snickered. "You better not, doc. She can't eat *normal* food. I spent a fortune on a *very* expensive meal for her, and she turned her nose up at it. Gave me some B.S story about silly-ass disease or something."

Unbelievable! If Kelly weren't fighting nausea and dizziness right now, she'd get up and strangle the man.

"Oh, is that right?" The doctor stopped in his tracks and looked concerned. "Are you saying you're Celiac?"

"Yes!" Kelly nodded.

"How long?"

"Since I was a kid. I can't eat wheat, barley, or rye."

"Are you familiar with cross-contamination?"

Kelly told him she did. She couldn't even have a bread crumb or she'd react. Cross-contamination was the biggest issue regarding the disease.

People don't realize it's not only about being gluten-free, it's about how it's made. If the same utensils used with foods containing gluten are used with gluten-free food, that's all it takes to make her sick.

Even spices use wheat flour as filler. Once, she found

wheat listed as an ingredient in electrolyte powder. It's terribly misunderstood. Kelly stopped trying to educate people about it a long time ago. All that leads to is shaming, misunderstanding, or outright denial. Especially since Hollywood makes people think it's just a health choice. Well, for her, it's not a choice, it's an actual necessity.

"What's this got to do with anything?" Parker scoffed with arms crossed in front of his chest. "Can't you see she's milking it?"

"Young man!" the doctor interrupted, "If you really are her boyfriend, you need to shut up and listen to her."

"I beg your pardon?" Parker looked like a bulldog ready to fight.

"My own daughter has Celiac Disease," the doctor told him. "She goes through hell. She's even got neurological symptoms. It's an autoimmune condition, and it's very debilitating. Have some respect!"

"Aw, that's a bunch of malarkey!" Parker scoffed. "There's no such thing as silly-ass disease! People go gluten-free because they think it's cool. It's just a fad. They're hypochondriacs. You know, it's all in the head! Demonizing perfectly good food like that is ridiculous! What a joke!"

"*Ma'am!*" the doctor motioned for Tweety to get the guy out of there. He turned back to Kelly and continued to examine her neck and glands for swelling.

"Right!" Tweety got up and hobbled to her grandson. She took his arm and tried to lead him out. "Let's you and me go take a walk."

"I'll go when I'm good and ready!" he yanked his arm away from her like a spoiled child.

Kelly knew one thing. A narcissist did not like to be put in his place.

"Could it be you ate something with gluten on the ship?"

"Maybe," she told the doctor, "But I only ate from the gluten-free table."

"Well, that's not always safe for Celiacs. People tend to cross-contaminate utensils. I'll see to it that you get Celiac-Safe gluten-free meals delivered to your stateroom for the rest of the cruise. We have a special kitchen for that with designated fryers and everything."

Kelly nodded. She was thankful for his help and concern.

"Can I ask what symptoms you get when you're glutened?"

"Um, usually my gut hurts and bloats out, but I've gotten vertigo from eating gluten in the past. I get this terrible back pain, and my throat and glands swell up. I've had a few anaphylactic reactions lately. My doctor gave me an EpiPen for that. Sometimes I even look like I'm drunk. People don't understand. Most of the time, they don't believe me."

The doctor reassured her, "Well, I do! I'll have a bottle of Gluten-Gone delivered to you tonight. It will help alleviate your symptoms. I'm pretty sure that's what's going on here, especially since the anti-nausea pills did not affect you. And one more thing. Your glands are very swollen under your jaw, and your neck is swollen too. I'll give you a shot of epinephrine to take the inflammation down."

"You gotta be kidding me!" Parker scoffed, "What a faker!"

Tweety shook her head.

"And you, young man, are out of line!" the doctor spat back, rising immediately to confront Parker. "Leave NOW!"

"Well, she's not coming with us tomorrow, then!" Parker eyed his grandmother. "I won't let her!"

"Honestly," the doctor turned to Kelly, "I wouldn't recommend going on any kind of strenuous excursions tomorrow. Maybe just stick around Juneau. They have a hospital if you need it, and there is plenty to do and see there if you feel up to it."

Kelly wanted to cry. She had already e-transferred Parker the money for the guided tour into bear country. She doubted he'd give it back. He already told her it was non-refundable.

All she wanted was for everyone to leave her alone. She never should've come on a trip like this by herself. It was a mistake. Maybe this was her wake-up call? She could fly home from Juneau tomorrow.

"My dear," Tweety turned to Kelly, "we'll talk tomorrow. Get a good night's sleep. Maybe you'll feel better in the morning. I'd still like you to come if you feel up to it."

"She's NOT coming, grandmother!"

Tweety took her grandson by the arm. This time, she was successful in leading him out, with the help of the doctor, of course.

After the doctor finished with her, he and Tweety left. The door locked behind them, and tears flooded her eyes. She didn't know what to do. All she wanted was to go home. The whole ordeal was very embarrassing!

Kelly glanced at the brown leather Bible that came with the room. She grabbed it from the nightstand, held it to her chest, and bawled like a baby. For the first time ever, she felt compelled to pray. It was the only thing she had left to try.

It reminded her of her Nana's Bible. Growing up, she taught her about God. It was never something she took seriously, though. In fact, Kelly always said she didn't believe in all that mumbo-jumbo. She thought it was important for some people, but not for her. Maybe she was wrong.

Okay, Nana, she decided. *I'll try it your way.*

Clearing her throat, she prayed, "God? If there is any God, please help me!"

Suddenly, a strange warmth overcame her. She sat up and started feeling a little bit better. Maybe it was the epinephrine the doctor gave her. Maybe it wasn't. *God? Is that you?*

There, lying on her stateroom bed, *something* seemed to comfort her. The dizziness was gone. Memories that plagued her seemed a little less painful. She felt at peace for the first time in a long time.

This was definitely not nothing!

JUST BREATHE

Morning shone brightly through the porthole window in Kelly's stateroom. She couldn't believe she had slept through the entire night. Should she chance lifting her head off the pillow?

Sometimes the dizziness seemed to be delayed. She could be fully sitting upright for a minute, then suddenly feel like the entire room was spinning.

Kelly took a breath and tried to sit up. She sat in her underwear at the edge of her bed. Nothing. She took another breath and waited. Still nothing.

Was she really better?

Little by little, Kelly turned her head from side to side. No dizziness, no nausea. In fact, she felt normal. She didn't seem to be affected anymore by accidentally coming in contact with gluten.

Suddenly, someone knocked at the door: "Room service!"

Kelly cautiously lifted her body from the bed and grabbed the white robe the cruise ship supplied. She took a breath and tied it around her waist.

"Coming!"

Shuffling slowly toward the door, she opened it to a smiling young man carrying a tray, "Ma'am…your breakfast."

Kelly nearly cried.

The young gentleman wore gloves, holding the tray with experience. The meal was completely sealed, and she could tell great care was put into the preparation of her meal.

"Doctor's orders," the young man said, "you have a completely Celiac-safe meal with no cross-contamination."

"Just a sec," Kelly shuffled to her purse to get some cash, "I have something for you."

"No need, Ma'am! The doctor took care of all the gratuities." He gave her the tray and bowed as he left the room.

How wonderful is that? Kelly was so thrilled to be pampered like this. It meant a lot to her. She made a mental note to thank the doctor. In fact, she would make sure she bought him something extra special at the next port.

Which reminded her. They were scheduled to arrive in Juneau by noon. It was nine-thirty now, so that meant she only had a few hours to get cleaned up before the ship docked.

Kelly unwrapped the delicious-looking meal of avocado on gluten-free toast, topped with a poached egg. Yum! This was going to be good. She sat down at the table and gobbled it down.

Oh, that felt wonderful. No nausea at all.

She gazed through the porthole expecting to see open ocean, but instead, she could see brightly coloured houses of yellow, blue, green, and red, on a hillside. Were they already in Juneau?

The ship was early. *Oh no!*

She would have to move it if she was going to meet up with the Masons for the bear tour. There was no way she was letting Parker win. She was going on this excursion whether he liked it or not.

Kelly looked at her watch. Luckily, the meeting time for the tour was 1pm at the Juneau Tramway building. From there, the guide would take them to the floatplane they were flying out on.

For a moment, the thought of flying brought her back to last night. Wasn't she going to fly home today? Hadn't she had enough? Yet, for some reason, she didn't feel like that anymore. Instead, she felt liberated, as if she could take on the world.

God? Is that you?

There was no other explanation. Since her prayer last night, she felt calmer than usual. Not like she was about to have a panic attack every time she turned around. That in itself was a miracle.

"Thank you, God!" Kelly decided to say out loud as she

looked up. "I-I really don't know what to say. I'm not used to talking to something I can't see, so excuse me if I sound like an idiot."

Kelly took a breath and smiled.

Maybe for the first time in a long time, she felt like things were going to work out. One thing was for sure: she was going to stop criticizing herself. She felt something tug at her heart just then. It told her she wasn't an idiot.

Why did she have to put herself down anyway? Even if others didn't hear it, she did. It happened all the time.

She'd look in the mirror and call herself ugly. She'd mess up at work and mentally call herself dumb. Confidence was somewhat limited most of the time. Well, this ends now.

Something seemed different somehow. Today, she would hold her head up high. Today, she would feel like she belongs. Not like an impostor. Not like a third wheel, which she repeatedly told herself she was, hanging around the Masons.

No, she was a strong, independent woman for going on this vacation alone. She would be positive about herself from here on in.

There was no way that idiot, Parker, was going to humiliate her again. In fact, she was going to deliberately be nice to him, just to show she was more emotionally intelligent than he was.

Kelly grabbed the backpack she purchased at one of the shops on the cruise ship and started stuffing it for the five-hour excursion ahead.

Just about everything she owned right now was purchased on the ship. It was like a little city. So many shops, just like downtown Toronto. It was incredible that they could manage to squeeze it all into one ship.

Perhaps one day, she would find the luggage she accidentally left at the Vancouver airport. It will probably be waiting for her in the unclaimed section once she returns there for her flight home. At least she was hoping it would.

After a quick shower, Kelly threw on a pair of jeans, a t-shirt, and her blue Alaska hoodie she bought in Ketchikan. It was so cozy and warm. She laced up her navy hiking boots she purchased specifically for this adventure. She was prepared.

Nothing was going to stop her from going on this bear tour. She felt completely better. A far cry from last night.

She was ready to meet up with the Masons, thankful for their friendship.

God, give me strength! It's Parker I need help with!

RIGHT OR WRONG

YOU ARE NOT COMING!" the mean voice shouted as Kelly approached the Masons standing with their gear.

Parker was like a mad dog, baring his teeth. He stood there with his hands on his hips, ready for a fight.

God, give me strength!

"*I AM TOO!*" she said, flipping her hair back.

Remember, be nice! A voice inside her head reminded her.

Chester stood there with a worried look on his face. Tweety just frowned. She immediately told Parker to cool it.

"I feel fine," Kelly told him.

"It doesn't matter if you feel fine. You're NOT spoiling it for him!"

"Parker, can we talk over here?" She nodded for him to meet down the hall a bit, away from Chester and Tweety's big ears. They walked in silence for a moment and then stopped in place.

She leaned in close to whisper to him, hoping he'd like her advancement. It was the only tactic she thought would work. Plus, it was a way to make amends.

Parker stood there, arms crossed, smelling like expensive cologne. His dark, handsome features were more apparent to her up close. It made her feel awkward. But then, she remembered she would practice confidence.

"Look," she whispered, "can we call a truce? I want to apologize."

"So, you admit you're a drunk?"

"What? NO!"

"Then we have nothing more to discuss!" he said, as he attempted to walk away from her.

"Wait, fine," she said, "I-I *am* a drunk." Kelly regretted the lie the moment it came out of her mouth. How could she say she was a drunk when it was the furthest thing from the truth?

Parker just stared at her with his piercing, dark eyes and pursed, well-formed lips. His chiselled jaw and clean-shaven face looked back at her as if he didn't believe her at all, not one single word.

What did he expect? Didn't he want her to admit it?

Even if it wasn't true, Kelly had to do something to appease the man. Of course, she didn't want to ruin it for Chester. Who was she to upset a dying man? She'd back out of it if it meant the old man would be happier without her going along. But not if it was just Parker being a jerk.

She knew how to soothe a narcissist. She wrestled with the thought of it, but realized it must be done.

"I knew you were a liar!" Parker shook his head in disgust.

Kelly sighed, deciding this was the point of no return. She'd pour it on thick now. "I know you did," she moved closer to him and put her hand on his chest.

Parker stood there liking it.

"You are pretty smart, I give you that," she buttered him up. "I'm sure that's why you're a lawyer. Do you have your own practice?"

"Yah, of course I do!"

Hook, line, and sinker. It was the only way. They had to be at the Tramway building in thirty minutes, and she was running out of time. She'd have to push harder.

"Tell me about your practice."

"Well, I earned my way to the top. I win all my cases, just so you know. My reputation is, well, let's just say you couldn't afford me, honey!"

"Oh, I'm sure I couldn't. You sound like one of the best. I could tell that about you the moment I saw you, and that handsome face of yours, you look pretty suave."

"You think so?" he grabbed his jaw and posed.

"Yah, you've got a certain charm about you, I must admit," Kelly played it up. "Even though we got off on the wrong foot, I kind of feel a tiny bit of an attraction toward you." *Oh, why did she say that? There's no turning back now.*

"I knew it! You like me!"

"Well…I said a *tiny* bit!" Kelly blushed.

She could see from the corner of her eye, Tweety waving them over and Chester pointing to his watch. Time was ticking.

"I think they're calling us back," Kelly chuckled.

"Let them wait. This is more important."

"No, seriously," Kelly showed him the time, "we have less than thirty minutes to meet up with the tour guide."

"Honey! Do you honestly think the guy will go without us? I paid big bucks for this guiding expedition. He's not going without us. He'll wait, believe me, he'll wait."

"I paid too."

"Yah-yah!" Parker dismissed it like it was nothing. "Anyhoo… Now that you've come to your senses, how about we make it official and you come as my date?"

What? This was not happening.

"I-um. What do you mean…exactly?"

"Well, blondie," he winked, "you know you can't resist me. That's why we've been fighting like cats and dogs. See, women always react like this toward me. They can't help it. You know… It's this face, like you said."

Oh boy, she fed his ego pretty good. It was sickening!

"Anyway, you owe me for last night," he told her point-blank. "So… What do you say? Is it a date?"

Time was ticking. It was either this or no tour.

Kelly sighed. She had no choice but to say yes. If it were the only way, she'd have to do it. She'd have to play the part. She was a good actress. Even if part of her wasn't acting and she really was attracted to him, she didn't want a relationship. She was never going to date a narcissist ever again! *Get it out of your head, girl, NO!*

Why was she always attracted to the wrong guy?

God, help me!

Chester and Tweety were jigging up and down like

impatient children. They wanted to go, and they wanted to go now. "Hurry up, you two," Tweety called down the corridor.

Parker held up an index finger, "We're coming!" He locked Kelly into a charming gaze and asked, "Well, what do you say?"

Her tender blue eyes couldn't focus, and she darted them away. Still, he waited for a response. Kelly knew she was in trouble now. He held both of her hands and asked her one more time, "Is it a date?"

"Fine! I guess so," she smirked, though she had no idea why, "It's a date then."

"Good! Now, just one more thing," Parker tapped his lips with his finger, "make it official. *Kiss me!*"

Wait! What?

Sure, she was attracted to him, but this was crossing the line. Nobody said anything about any physical contact, yet she started it. She's the one who made advancements by putting her hand on his chest.

It was all her fault.

She bit her lip and wondered how she could get out of this one.

Then, impulsively, he leaned forward and gave her a sloppy, wet kiss. It was all over the place, and she hated it.

Yet, she kind of liked it too. *Uh, oh!*

What on earth was she going to do now?

The two of them wandered over to Chester and Tweety, holding hands, blushing and smiling.

Why was she smiling? She had no clue.

"I told you, Tweety-Bird!" Chester broke out in a laugh.

"No, you didn't!"

"Yes, I did."

Parker rolled his eyes. "You two," he chuckled. "See, babe, opposites do attract!"

It sure was the opposite. It was the complete opposite of what she meant to happen, yet, for some reason, she found herself liking it, at least the part that made her feel accepted. Liked. Loved by another man again, even if it was going to be short-lived.

Right or wrong, good or bad, Kelly decided she would enjoy the date, at least for today. Tomorrow would be a different story.

Now, all they had to do was get to the Tramway building on time.

TIME TO FLY

Boone couldn't believe he slept in. That's what he gets for forgetting his phone at the hospital. It must be there. He already turned the house upside down, and it's not anywhere. He even took a look at Mary's, and he didn't leave it there last night either.

He has to drop by the hospital before his tour starts anyway. Even though he was running late, he wanted to make time. Mary was important to him. He wanted to make sure she was going to be okay before taking off for five hours.

He'll skip the gear-check and the pre-flight prep and do it when the guests arrive. *Sometimes, you've gotta make exceptions,* he told himself. He didn't like doing that, but one time wouldn't hurt.

Hopefully, this group will be more mature than the last group. He didn't want any trouble, and he certainly didn't want a mess again. The plane still smelled a little rank even though the boys sanitized it pretty well.

One thing caught him off guard. The Sunshine Liner docked earlier than expected, and that meant there would be tourists all over town already. He had better get going, so there would be no unexpected delays. Traffic wasn't usually a problem in Juneau, but it would still be busy. The last thing he wanted was to be late for his own tour.

By the time Boone got to the hospital, it was already noon. Mary wasn't in her room. What was going on?

"Excuse me," Boone asked a nurse in the hall, "I'm looking for Mary. She's not in her room."

"Oh, she's in surgery."

Boone felt his heart sink. "For what?"

"She's getting her gallbladder removed. It's emergency surgery. The surgeon took her right in. She was in a lot of pain this morning, and the test results confirmed it was the gallbladder. Are you a relative?"

"I'm the only one she's got."

"You were here last night, then?"

"Yes. Do you know how long the surgery is?" Boone looked worried. He didn't want to leave without knowing if she would be okay. Could he cancel the tour? Was that even possible at this point?

"She's been in surgery for about an hour. It's usually a one-to-two-hour surgery if there are no complications."

"Okay, thanks for letting me know. Is it okay to just wait in her room?"

"That would be fine," the nurse nodded, "I'll come and give you an update as soon as I hear anything."

Boone entered her room and looked around. His cell phone had to be somewhere. Finding it was his first priority. He had some phone calls to make. He'd have to get the boys to meet up with the group and bring them down to the plane. Hopefully, they were available.

Where is that thing? Could someone have stolen it? He hoped not. It had all his permits and itinerary for the group today. Sure, the permits were on record, but from experience, he always kept them with him just in case.

Lord? Help me find it. And while I'm praying, help Mary to be okay through her surgery. And get me out of here on time for my tour.

Boone looked under the covers. He looked under the bed. He looked in the bathroom. The phone was nowhere to be found. What was he going to do without it?

"Excuse me, miss," Boone asked housekeeping nearby, "hello?"

She looked at him and removed her earbuds, "Sorry, did you say something?"

"Yes, I was wondering if anyone had found a cell phone in here. It's a black Samsung."

"I just got on shift. I can check with my supervisor. Or, maybe the nurse will know. You should ask her."

"I'd appreciate it if you'd check with your supervisor and let me know as soon as possible. I'll also ask the nurse."

She nodded and left the room.

"Excuse me, nurse?" he asked at the station nearby, "I lost my cell phone. Did you happen to see a black Samsung in Mary's room?"

"No, I don't think so. At least nobody said anything to me. I'll ask around, but I don't think so. Do you need to call someone?"

"Yes, urgently! Do you have a cell phone I could borrow?"

"Well, not a cell phone, but there's a land line you can use over there," she pointed to one on the wall.

Landline? How was he supposed to text the boys with that? He didn't even know hospitals had landlines anymore.

"You don't happen to have a cell phone I could borrow, do you? I need to text someone." Teenagers don't talk on the phone these days. He usually texted the boys when he needed them. He didn't think he'd ever talked to them over the phone before.

"Sorry, I would if I could," she said. "They're work phones, and it's against regulations to let patients use them."

Boone sighed and headed for the archaic landline. Did he even remember the boys' numbers? He had to think for a moment. What was it?

An old man wheeled over to him, distracting him for a moment. He had a broken leg that stuck out, bumping into things. He got it stuck in a corner and asked for help.

"Excuse please," he said in broken English like Mary. "Me need help! You help?"

Boone smiled and set the phone back on the receiver. He couldn't remember the number at the moment anyway. The old man made him think of Mary. He wondered how her surgery was going.

"No problem," he told the old guy. "Let me help you there, buddy."

Just as Boone grabbed the handles of the man's wheelchair, he saw a black phone peeking out of the side of his chair. "Is that your phone?"

The old man suddenly put his shaky hand over it. "Mine!"

"Can I just see it for a moment?"

"No!"

Boone knew by the cross sticker on the case that it was his phone. How could he get it away from the guy?

Thank you, Lord, for helping me find it! Now help me get it back.

The old guy gripped the phone firmly. He held it to his body and would not let go. "Sir, I need to see your phone."

"NO! Me phone!"

There was no getting the phone away from this guy. Maybe a nurse could help. He scoured the room to look for one, but nobody was around now, not even housekeeping.

At least he knew where his phone was. Now he needed to go find a nurse to help him get it back.

Boone excused himself and took off down the hallway.

It was bright and sunny outside, and from his vantage point, he could see the enormous Sunshine Liner docked in the distance. It was a reminder that he had to hurry. He only had thirty minutes before he had to meet his group.

And what about Mary?

He walked by the surgery doors and wondered if he could get an update. Nobody was around, and he knew better than to go through those doors without permission.

Suddenly, an O.R. nurse burst through the surgery doors. He stopped her mid-flight, "Excuse me? Can you tell me how Mary's doing?"

"Who?"

"The gallbladder surgery."

"Um, I think they're done. I'm just a scrub nurse, though. You should really talk to the surgeon."

This was good news. Maybe he'd be out of there on time after all.

Another nurse whizzed by. It was the one he talked to

earlier. Good, he needed to talk to her. "Excuse me? Remember me?"

He hoped she wouldn't think he was stalking her.

"I sure do!" she said. She was so cheerful. He really appreciated people who did their jobs well. It was rare to find a caring spirit these days. It's something he hoped to bring into his own business.

"I hate to bother you, but I found my cell phone. An old guy with a broken leg seems to think it's his."

"Oh, that would be Barney," she laughed. "We couldn't get him out of Mary's room this morning. He was so concerned when she was crying in pain. It was sweet."

Crying in pain? And where was he? Sleeping. Boone couldn't help but feel a twinge of shame. He should have been there earlier.

"I'll get the phone back, don't you worry," she told him as she started to walk in the other direction. It looked like she was quite busy.

He hated to be a pain. "You know, if you don't mind, I really need it now. It's urgent that I text someone…like now!"

"Oh okay, well, let me just go to the bathroom first and I'll be right there."

"Of course," How could he be so insensitive? These nurses were run off their feet. They didn't even have time to use the bathroom, let alone get a cellphone from an old guy.

Boone went back to Mary's room and decided to just wait. There was nothing more he could do to speed things up. It was something he learned in prison. As much as he wanted his sentence to go quickly, he had to see it through.

Just like now.

It was a hard thing to learn, but something the Lord was still working on him with. He definitely was a work in progress.

It was already 1 pm. He was officially not going to make his tour on time. Hopefully, the nurse wouldn't be too much longer.

Finally, after about fifteen minutes, the nurse skipped into the room and brought him his cell phone. "You're right, Barney did not want to give it up. It turns out he thought it was Mary's and he was keeping it safe for her until she got out of surgery. What a sweet guy!"

"Thank you so much!" Boone really appreciated her kindness. Now he could text the boys and hope they could meet the group right away. They were only about five minutes away.

"Oh, and Mary is out of surgery and in recovery. She's doing great. I went to check on her first. That's what took me so long."

"Thank you again! You're a good nurse."

She smiled and thanked him, then went on her way.

Boone opened his contacts and texted the older boy. He asked him if he and his brother could go to the Tramway and meet the group and bring them over to the plane. He'd be there in half an hour.

"We sure can, boss," the boy texted back immediately, "but that'll cost you." He added several smiley faces.

"No problem!" Boone texted back, "You guys are a lifesaver!"

Once they wheeled Mary back into her room and talked to her to make sure she was okay, he headed out the door. He explained what he had to do, and Mary, being the kindhearted person she was, told him he had better go do that then.

Quickly, he headed out the door to his car and fired it up. He needed to get to the seaplane dock in a hurry.

It's time to fly!

THE GINGER

Luckily, the Tramway building was only a short walk from where their cruise ship docked. The group arrived just in time. It was nearly 1 pm.

Kelly wished she had time to take the scenic Tram up the mountain. From what she researched, it was a main attraction in Juneau. There were even hiking trails, a gift shop and a gallery.

She could even watch a short film about the first indigenous people of the Pacific Northwest. The Tlingit people fascinated her. She loved learning about their culture. That's why she purchased the native dress she wore last night.

Memories of her wearing it haunted her. *That thing you're wearing!* His criticism still stung. How could she just let something like that go? He knew what he was saying. But then, she was trying to be nicer to him. Maybe if she smothered him with kindness, he would turn over a new leaf.

Not likely!

She should be downright angry about that. Yet, for some reason, her decision to go along as his date showed the opposite. What on earth was she doing?

Tweety told Chester to go sit on a bench, and then nodded to her grandson. The two of them went to talk. Kelly silently followed behind them.

"Where is this guy?" Parker complained as he looked at his watch. "I invested a lot of money and time into this, Gram."

"I know you did, Honey," Tweety said. "Just keep your voice down. I don't want to upset your grandfather. He's got enough on his mind."

The place was bustling with visitors. It was a busy destination for the middle of June. The bright, warm sunshine helped a great deal. It was finally warm enough to go without a jacket. Kelly wondered now if she should have brought along a hat and sunscreen. She didn't expect the weather to be this nice. Yet, she was told to prepare for all types of weather. It changes quickly around here.

Kelly didn't want to let Parker spoil the mood for everyone. If they had already paid for the excursion, surely the guide would show up. How could he not? Even though it was going on 1:30 pm now, she wasn't worried. It was warm. It was sunny. She was in Alaska and ready to enjoy the excursion of a lifetime. She even purchased a camera to capture the bears. Sure she could use her cell phone, but the Panasonic camera she bought was well worth it. Besides, she had been meaning to get a *real* camera for months anyway.

"Did you try to call him?" Kelly butt into the conversation.

"Of course I did!" Parker barked at her. "What do you think, I'm dumb or something? *Geez!*"

Let it go!

She was not letting him ruin this. Nope! Tweety had already scolded him for that remark, anyway. He was quite agitated. Granted, he had good reason. If a tour guide says he's going to meet you at a certain time, generally, he shows up.

The group went over to join Chester on the bench. Parker looked at his watch again and sighed. She could tell he was trying to keep his mouth shut, but the grimace on his face was way worse. It was comical. The man looked like a pouting, spoiled child.

Kelly tried to hold his hand to reassure him, but he just pulled away and shook his head. She dealt with this kind of tantrum before when Ted tried to pull it. If one remedy didn't work, there were *other* solutions she could try to calm him down. She wrapped both arms around his muscular bicep and leaned her head against his shoulder. "We can find other things to do while we wait, can't we?"

That changed his sulky mood.

"Why not!" Parker smirked, "Give me a kiss then."

Against her better judgment, she did just what he asked. The performance was epic.

What are you doing, Kelly? Her thoughts bombarded her. Of course, she ignored them and continued to console him. After all, the show would amuse Chester and change the mood for everyone. Wasn't that what needed to happen here?

Tweety was not impressed.

Suddenly, from around the corner, two teenage boys asked for Parker Mason. He rose immediately. They apologized profusely for the delay and took turns shaking his hand like he was a celebrity. "Good afternoon, bear watchers! Welcome to Second Chance Bear Guides!"

Kelly helped Chester and Tweety get on their feet. It was a relief that they were finally going to start the tour. Parker was busy walking ahead with the boys. It looked like he was scolding them. She knew that was likely what was happening and hoped he wouldn't be too hard on them. They seemed to be kind-hearted young boys.

Nate and Liam were their names. They led them to the floatplane down at the docks. "Our boss is running a bit late," Liam told the group. "We apologize again for the delay. "He had an emergency at the hospital, but he's on his way now. If you can all climb into the plane one by one, my brother Nate and I will help you up. As requested, only one backpack is allowed. You can keep it under your seat. There's plenty of room."

They helped Chester up first. It was quite an ordeal to get him into the plane, but he finally sat comfortably. His smile said it all. There were tears of joy as he watched Tweety climb up, with some assistance, of course.

"After you!" Parker waved her to go first.

Progress! Maybe he could act like a gentleman after all.

"I haven't been in one of these kinds of planes before!" Kelly beamed, excited for the ride. The two young teenagers pointed to her seat. They placed her backpack under it and turned to Parker. "Do you need a hand?"

"I can do it myself!"

80

The boys backed away from him. He must have really let them have it. They were being polite, but Kelly could tell they didn't really want to help him anyway. He was rude and miserable to them.

"What is that rank smell?" Parker complained as he sat in his seat. "It smells worse than an outhouse!"

The boys turned to each other and grimaced. "We're sorry," they said, "we sanitized the plane as best we could."

"Unbelievable! This is the worst experience I've ever had. You guys are…"

"Are what, great employees?" a voice interrupted from behind. He was a good-looking ginger-haired man with a well-manicured red beard and tattoos up and down both arms. He had a wrestler-type body that made Parker's physique pale in comparison.

"And this would be our boss!" Nate said as he turned to introduce him. "Ladies and gentlemen," Liam continued, where Nate left off, "this is bear guide extraordinaire. The legendary Boone McKenzie. He's also the pilot."

"Pleased to meet you folks! Apologies for being late. I had an emergency. I hope the boys gave you the royal treatment."

Kelly couldn't help but smile and blush. She had never met a redheaded man before. It was odd, but the truth. Most gingers were women, in her opinion. It was rare to find a ginger man. She chuckled to herself, thinking of *the gingerbread man.* His red and black checkered shirt suited him so well, and the cut-off sleeves showed off his muscles.

Parker scowled at her. She guessed because she noticed how handsome he was.

Chester and Tweety introduced themselves. They reached out a hand to the gorgeous lumberjack. He lifted himself into the plane with ease. Parker gave him a fishy handshake, and Kelly fumbled her words. "I-I'm Pelly Keston…I-I mean…Kelly Preston."

"Don't mind her," Parker joked, "my girlfriend drinks too much."

Kelly did a double-take. Her annoyance was obvious. Tweety piped up before she could say a word. "Don't mind our grandson. He thinks he's a judge but he's really just a lawyer." She made a clown face that de-escalated the situation. Only grandmothers knew how to do that.

"Just a lawyer? Come on, Gram, you're killing me!"

"Well, pleased to meet you all," the handsome redhead interrupted. "I have a pre-flight check to do first, and then we'll be on our way."

Everyone cheered.

Kelly was fuming. She unzipped her backpack and rummaged through it, pretending to look for something.

She zipped it back up and set it down. From the corner of her eye, she could see Parker glaring at her. She folded her arms in defiance. She was not looking at him!

What a jerk!

SHUT UP!

The boys helped Boone do the outside pre-flight check so it would go faster. They inspected the floats for damage, combing through every part of the hollow red and white pontoons, including the rudders.

They inspected the three-blade propeller. The wings. It all looked good. He gave both boys a hundred-dollar bill each and sent them on their way. He was very grateful to have their help.

All he had left to do was check the fuel and oil levels and make sure the flight controls were working properly.

He hefted himself into the cockpit and put his Bose aviation headset on his head, and plugged it in. It was well worth the investment. After the old ones his dad used fell apart, he decided to upgrade.

"Everyone!" Boone announced, "If you haven't found them yet, please put on your headsets. It's how we'll be able to talk in-flight."

Boone pointed to the mic and showed them the controls. He didn't want to start the engine until everyone was ready.

They all nodded!

The giant red and white seaplane roared to life. The passenger's eyes grew wide with excitement, and now he could do his inside pre-flight check and make sure the flight controls were working.

"Okay, people, listen up!" Boone talked through his high-quality mic so they could all hear him. "Let's everyone say hello, and your name, so I can make sure things are working. Then I'll continue."

Each person on board introduced themselves, and Boone nodded at them one by one. "Great! Looks like we're all set. But first, we have a bit of housekeeping to do."

"You got that right! It sure stinks in here!" the rude younger man complained through his headset.

"Sorry, folks," Boone apologized, "the last group couldn't keep their lunch down. We sanitize after every tour, though, so if there's any kind of mess still, other than a slight smell, please let me know."

"Slight smell, my foot," the young man scoffed.

There was always a troublemaker or a wise-guy in the group. Boone had his eye on him. He'd put him in his place if he had to. This time, he was not putting up with any B.S.

"I see you all brought light-weight carry-ons with you. Great! That is the only allowable baggage in the cabin. Anything else goes inside the cargo hold. I hope none of you have bear spray in your bags. I don't allow that on my plane. I have some safely stored in the cargo hold. You each get one once we land. Do I need to ask if you have open bear spray again?"

They all said no.

"Good! Then let's go over some safety rules, shall we? First, everyone must wear seatbelts. Do not remove them until I tell you. Even once we land, you must keep them on until we come to a full stop. I'll let you know when it's safe."

The group sat there and listened intently.

"Second, the emergency exists are there," he pointed out. "Your life preservers are there. NEVER INFLATE THEM INSIDE THE AIRCRAFT! Got it?"

They nodded.

Boone paused for a moment, hoping he wasn't scaring them. Sometimes he did, especially with the next part.

"Great! The third and most important part...know how to get to safety if we crash."

The two women gasped.

"Always be prepared, because anything can happen when you fly. The most important thing to do is to stay calm. If we crash, we most likely will flip over. Release your seatbelt, find the exits, and get to the surface as quickly as possible. Once you have cleared the wreckage, only then is it safe to inflate your life preserver."

"Oh, come on! This guy is just trying to scare us!" a voice whispered through the headset.

Boone did a double-take. "Who said that?"

Everyone went silent.

"Sir?" he pointed to the young man, "Am I going to have trouble with you?"

The man laughed.

"What's so funny, buddy?"

"You are!" the rude man argued. "I didn't pay a fortune to have you scare the living daylights out of us."

"Outside! NOW!" Boone commanded. He dropped his headset and exited the cockpit. He walked around to the passenger door where the troublemaker exited, ready for a fight.

"Is this your plane?" Boone questioned him sternly.

The man shook his head.

"No, it's not. So, when you're on board MY plane, you do what I say. You respect what I say, and you do not question it. Your life could depend on it. Their lives could depend on it. Is that clear?"

The arrogant man saluted him.

"No no no...I don't appreciate that either. Either you respect me, or you can leave. I don't need your business, buddy."

Truthfully he did, but the bluff was worth it, just to see the guy squirm. He was supposed to be a big shot lawyer or something, but Boone didn't expect such juvenile behaviour from him. Not only was he rude to Nate and Liam earlier, but he was rude to his girlfriend as well.

The guy smirked like it was a big joke.

"Look, I don't need the lecture," he told Boone. "You think this is my first rodeo? I know all the silly safety rules already. You don't need to preach to the choir."

"Oh, you know all the rules, do you," Boone mocked. "Well first, the rules are not silly, they could save your life."

The troublemaker shrugged.

Tell me this, wise guy. Why don't you inflate a personal life preserver right away? Might as well get it ready early so you don't drown. Hey? Why on earth would you wait?"

"I wouldn't! You got it all wrong, pal!"

"Oh, I got it wrong? Well, here's a thought, *pal.* You don't inflate a PFD inside a seaplane because YOU CAN'T SWIM WITH IT UNDERWATER! Yeah, like I said, a plane flips when it crashes."

"Fine, buddy! You want a hero cookie or something?"

Boone couldn't believe the man. "An apology would be nice."

"Fine. Sorry! Now, can we just go? We're already late because of you."

Unbelievable!

Boone decided to let the last barb go. It wasn't worth risking the trip. Right now, he just wanted him to shut up.

"Go!" Boone pointed to the door and watched the man sheepishly climb back into the seaplane. He plopped himself into his seat and stared out the window. *Good riddance!*

Boone secured the door and climbed back into the cockpit as well. He put his headset back on and prepared to fly.

He wiped his brow and was glad it didn't go sideways.

"Juneau tower, November Five Eight Zero Delta Bravo, Cessna 180, North departure, requesting taxi, holding short of the waterline. Over."

The plane slowly inched forward, ready for takeoff. The buzz of the aircraft silenced everyone. It was the part of the trip Boone liked best. Open skies and a bright blue horizon.

Now all he had to do was answer their millions of questions as he pointed out the sights along the way. "Ready to go see some bears?"

Everyone cheered!

THE TALK

And that's Mendenhall Glacier," the pilot pointed below. It was gorgeous! Kelly leaned against the window and looked down. From her vantage point, she could see ice that looked like it was melting down a mountain face, and then froze in place. It was an absolutely incredible sight to see.

"It's so blue," she said.

Tweety was fascinated too. "Look at it, Chester!"

The pilot went on. "It's part of the Tongass National Forest. The Tlingit people first named it Sitaantaago. There are other names for it, but my mother can pronounce them better than I can. Her ancestors are Tlingit."

"You're Tlingit?" Kelly asked, surprised.

"I highly doubt that!" Parker scoffed, "he's a Scot, can't you tell?"

The man was still sulking from earlier. Up until now, he was as quiet as a mouse. She was embarrassed by the way he was acting.

"The fact is, I'm a half breed," the pilot told them. "My mother is as well, but she's part Tlingit on her mother's side. My grandmother is a pure Kootznoowoo-Tlingit from Angoon. I, unfortunately, take after my Scottish father. Growing up around my grandmother as a redhead with no pigment, was not fun. She always joked that I was adopted. *Not funny!*"

Parker shook his head like he didn't believe him, and then buried himself in a law textbook he brought along. Why anyone would be reading at a time like this was beyond her.

"Why don't you sit up front with me?" the pilot invited her. "You can see much better up here."

"Not on your life," Parker snapped back.

"Why not?"

Kelly gave Parker a dirty look. She didn't need his permission. She didn't owe him anything.

The pilot furrowed his brow and shook his head. "Maybe you want to come up here instead, buddy. How about that!" he grinned as he looked back at the man.

"No thanks!"

Kelly could feel her face turn red. She sat frozen in her seat. Why did she let Parker stop her? He wasn't really her boyfriend. Sure, she agreed to come along as his date, but the whole thing was a ruse. She barely knew the guy. She didn't owe him anything.

She paid her own way. This was her trip, too. And why couldn't she go sit with the pilot? What harm was there in that? The whole thing reminded her of Ted's jealousy.

"You know what?" Kelly turned to the pilot, "I think I'll take you up on that offer. Yup, I'm coming up there." She didn't even look at Parker.

The handsome redhead beamed.

Kelly unbuckled her seatbelt. She shimmied her way up to the front of the plane and sat beside the pilot. "I forgot your name."

"Boone."

He showed her how to have a one-on-one conversation through the headset. Nobody needed to hear what they were talking about anyway.

"And what was your name again? Pelly?" Boone laughed.

"Very funny!" she chuckled. Kelly was sure Parker was burning a hole in the back of her head right now, but she didn't care. She was going to enjoy this trip and Boone was interesting. A lot more interesting than the jerk of a lawyer sitting behind her.

"How long have you been with fancy-pants?"

Kelly looked back at Parker just to be sure he couldn't hear. She didn't know why she was so worried about it. Yet, something tugged at her heart. Part of her felt sorry for the idiot.

"He can't hear us."

Kelly bit her lip. "Look," she said, "he's not really my boyfriend. I only agreed to come along as his date. I just met the Masons on the cruise."

Boone grinned through his long red beard. "Okay. Well, I definitely wouldn't let there be a second date. In case you haven't noticed, the guy's a jerk."

"I-I guess."

"You guess? The pilot gasped. "Did he pay for your ticket, or did he make you pay?"

"Well, I paid, but…"

"And how much did he charge you?"

Kelly bit her lip again. "Two grand."

"Two grand?" the pilot threw his head back, "I only charge eleven hundred. He sure made a killing off of you."

Knowing that, Kelly choked, and tears started to well. Her heart began to beat fast, and she could feel a panic attack coming on. *NO!*

God, are you there?

Under her breath, she prayed God would calm her down like he did before. She must have been moving her mouth, unaware, because the pilot noticed.

"You praying?"

"I-um, yah," Kelly trembled. The guy was on to her, and she didn't expect that. He was so different from Ted, and Parker. He seemed to really care. His compassionate personality was refreshing. He was definitely not the kind of guy she usually found herself with.

"How long have you been a believer?"

Kelly stared blankly at him and paused. She didn't know what to say. All she knew was that she believed God had helped her last night. Now she talks to him. Does that make her a believer? She didn't really know.

"Um, well, I guess since last night."

The man smiled. "Are you serious? Well, *hallelujah!*"

Her Nana used that word. It warmed her soul to hear that.

She always thought it was an odd thing to say, but right now, it felt completely normal for some reason.

"I've been saved for a few years," he told her.

She was used to the lingo from her Nana talking about it all the time. In fact, she knew quite a bit about Christianity. She knew God sent Jesus Christ to save us from the consequences of sin. He bore our sins in his body and took the punishment for us, so we wouldn't have to. That was through his death and resurrection.

Kelly's Nana used to always say, We're *all sinners because it runs in our blood from Adam and Eve. That means we are all guilty. Even if you tell a little white lie, you're still a sinner who needs to be saved. Christ was a sacrificial lamb, so to speak. His blood covers over our sin and makes us clean.*

Most of the time, she rolled her eyes when her Nana gave her this kind of lecture. But she still listened to her every word. Only, she didn't know what to do with it all. It was just information.

Until now.

"Can I ask you something?" Kelly said.

"Shoot!"

"I'm new at this. I mean, I understand who God is and everything. My Nana drilled it into me growing up. But something feels different since last night. *I talk to God.* Is that normal?"

The pilot scratched his red beard. "Explain to me exactly what happened last night."

Kelly went on and explained the entire event, minus the embarrassing parts. She even told him about her panic attacks and how they seemed to stop.

"You know what it is?" the pilot told her point-blank, "it's a relationship."

"Yah, it's kind of like that. But it's weird, isn't it?"

"Not at all. Think of you and fancy-pants. In order for your relationship to progress, which I do *not* recommend by the way, you have to be honest with each other and talk. Not just about him, but about you too."

That's something she didn't have with Ted, or any man, for that matter. She sure didn't have it with Parker.

"To have a relationship with Jesus Christ, you have to communicate with Him. That means tell Him everything. Pour out your heart and tell Him all your problems. Pray continuously and read His word. The Bible. He talks to you that way."

"And people don't think you're nuts?"

"I'm sure they do," he chuckled, "but I don't care. He has never let me down like my old man did. A wise pastor once told me that Jesus is like a father to the fatherless. I didn't really have a good one, so that made sense to me."

Neither did she, but she didn't want to open up that whole can of worms right now.

"Cool. I was just wondering what other people's experiences were."

"Anytime. It sounds to me like you got the Holy Ghost last night. Don't be freaked out, but when you finally believe, like with your whole heart, not your head, Jesus gives you a gift. It's part of Him. It's called the Holy Spirit, and He'll help you through everything if you let Him. He'll even teach you. He's really the only teacher you'll ever need."

"So, that's it then? I'm a believer now?"

"Absolutely! The only qualification for Salvation is to believe. Most people complicate it and want to add works into the picture. That means they think they have to earn it, like a job or something. There ain't nothing we have to do to earn it. It's a free gift. It's simple enough for a child to understand. God intended it that way."

"Interesting."

"Now...you can go ahead and get baptized if you want, but only after the fact. It's meant to be a declaration of faith, that's it. It doesn't save you. You don't need to keep yourself saved by living like a saint either. Sure, we should try, but we fall short of the glory of God every single day. I know I do. He just keeps giving me grace. It ticks me off that people try to complicate Salvation. Just believe, and let the Holy Spirit do the rest."

Kelly nodded her head. She was glad she asked him about this. He definitely answered all her questions. He was so easy to talk to. She couldn't believe she even told him about her panic attacks.

"I like meeting baby Christians," the pilot told her, "And I don't mean it to be insulting. I just mean it's all brand new to you. It reminds me how good He is! Just keep talking to God, and He will guide you. Trust me on that one. I've been through the wringer."

She looked into his kind blue eyes and saw something there. Pain. Regret. She didn't want to ask. Maybe there would be an opportunity to finish this conversation sometime. For now, she was grateful for his wisdom. He sure was a breath of fresh air.

"Thank you, Boone," she smiled softly. Thank you for sharing all your wisdom with me. I really appreciate it."

"It has been my honour. Now I think you'd better get back to your seat. Looks like we've arrived at Admiralty Island.

"Buckle up everyone! We're here!"

THE ARRIVAL

The seaplane touched down on the east side of Admiralty Island at a place called Pack Creek. High mountain peaks and old-growth spruce set as a backdrop to one of the most pristine wilderness areas in Alaska.

Known for its high concentration of brown bears, Pack Creek is also home to Sitka black tailed deer, mink, river otters, and martens. The nesting bald eagles found on the island are also the highest population in the world.

Boone loved this place. The tidal flats alone made the trip worth it. Every time he looked at them, he was amazed. God broke the mould. The winding water pathways looked like a drained seabed at low tide. It looked like a beautiful postcard to him.

He'd live here if he could.

Fond memories flooded in. He spent numerous summers in Angoon visiting his grandmother. Then, again, as a teenager, learning to guide. He remembered pronouncing the name, *Kootznoowoo,* for the first time and butchering it while everyone laughed. Fortress of the Bear was much easier to say as a six-year-old with no two front teeth. In other words, it was the bear's home, and he respected that.

Boone knew the importance firsthand.

The hydrodynamic buoyancy of the floats and the rudder helped Boone get as close to shore as possible. They would have to wade through some water on foot, but not much. He had rubber boots in the back for everyone. At least it was a warm sunny day.

As the rusty red and white Cessna 180 slowly came to a stop, Boone was glad he chose the mouth of the creek. It would be the best location since the tide was low. The area was impacted by tidal fluctuations all the time, and getting out was something he also had to consider.

"Okay, crew," he told them, "You can take your seatbelts off now. Take your shoes off, too, and stuff them into a bag. We're going to have to wade in."

"But I don't have rubber boots," Kelly told him.

"Neither do we," the others complained.

"No worries. I have enough for everyone."

Boone jumped out of his door and splashed into the water with his hip waders he already had on. It was just below his knees. He threw the anchor in and headed for the port side door to the cargo hold.

It was an extra-large black tote with a yellow lid. It had to be there somewhere. He moved around other totes, but that one didn't seem to be there.

Could it be that the boys forgot that one? He knew he should have checked the gear. That's what he gets for trusting two teenage boys. As great as they are, they're still just boys. It was his responsibility to make sure all the gear was packed.

Oh boy! The bear spray was in that box, too.

Don't panic, Boone, he told himself.

Plan B. "Well, people, it looks like we don't have boots after all. I forgot the tote. It also had the bear spray in it."

Suddenly, he heard Parker complaining. "Great! That's incompetent, don't you think? What kind of tour guide are you, buddy? I want my money back!"

Boone glared at the arrogant man. "I'm sorry, guys. I'll take you on a bonus trip to Angoon after this to make up for it if you like."

He wasn't sure he had enough time to fly to the west side of the island, but he'd try. Sometimes he would surprise the tourists with a quick fly into Angoon. Going the extra mile brought five-star reviews, usually. In this case, it might just be a necessity.

"I don't know if we should still go see the bears," the gray-haired lady at the back told her husband. "They don't have bear spray."

"I'm going, Tweety! You can't stop me!" he told her as he inched out of his seat.

The guy was quite heated for some reason.

"Let's everyone roll up their pant legs. Take your socks off and we'll go barefoot through the water. It's warm out anyway. It won't take us long to get to shore."

Parker made trouble again. "That's easy for you to say, buddy. You've got the hip waders."

Boone sighed. "I can take these off if you want to wear them instead."

Mr. Fancy Pants shook his head. That's what he thought. He just wanted to stir up trouble. He knew plenty of guys like him in prison. Nothing he said or did would matter. Boone was just going to have to ignore his rudeness for the rest of the trip.

Second Chance Bear Guides didn't give refunds anyway.

One by one, Boone helped his passengers step into the cold Alaskan water. He could see two rangers standing on the shoreline, ready for them to come in. It was Jack and Liz on duty. He hadn't seen those two in a long time, especially Liz.

It didn't take more than a few minutes to get to shore. They all waded through the water quite easily. Everyone seemed happy, except for Parker. He sat on a rock and put his socks and shoes back on immediately.

Who brings dress shoes on a bear guide? He was ridiculous with his black dress pants and white dress shirt. He looked like he was ready for court, not hiking.

"Welcome to Pack Creek, everyone!" Ranger Jack greeted each person individually while Liz did the same. "Once you're all ready, we'll go over some safety rules before Boone takes you off to see the bears."

"You guys are lucky!" Ranger Liz smiled. "Boone McKenzie is a legend around here. He's one of the locals. Don't let that red hair and blue eyes fool you. He's as Tlingit as it gets."

Boone quickly refused the compliment. It made him uneasy.

He wasn't one to puff himself up. "Okay, okay, these guys are the real heroes."

Liz was his high-school sweetheart back in his innocent years. These days, he tries to keep his nose clean when it comes to women. Sure, he had a few girlfriends before her but, she was his one-and-only a lifetime ago, before he went to jail. They went their separate ways soon after he got out. Now, since Jesus, it has been hard to find someone who has the same faith and morals. He knew she did not.

"Okay, listen up!" Ranger Jack quieted them, "First things first. We need to see everyone's ID so we can make sure you have a valid permit. As you know, you can't get in without one."

Everyone pulled out their ID from their backpacks. Boone brought his phone over to Jack to show him the permits. "Should be a piece of cake. All four are accounted for."

Chester and Tweety Mason showed their ID. Ranger Jack nodded. Then Parker Mason showed his ID. Ranger Jack nodded again. When Boone pulled up the last one, he stumbled over the name.

"Sara Price?" he furrowed his brow. "Do you go by Sara? I thought your name was Kelly Preston."

Then the blonde sheepishly bit her lip and told him the truth. "I'm not Sara." She looked worried. "I-I'm Kelly. Is there a problem, Ranger Jack?"

"Yes, there's a problem. Permits are not transferable."

Boone tore his ball cap off and raked his fingers through his red hair. He should have caught this. Had he not been in such a hurry this morning, he would have had time to check things over. He knew what this meant.

Kelly looked frustrated. Boone honestly felt sorry for her. The rangers were not going to let her in. This happened to him and his dad only once, and it was something he'd never forget. The people got so upset that they were refused entry, and they forced his dad to give them their money back. Not only that, but his dad's business reputation suffered because of their bad mouthing of the business.

"You three can go with Boone, but she can't go to the viewing tower, sand spit, or estuary," Ranger Jack told them all.

Suddenly, Parker threw his head back and began laughing hysterically. "This is priceless!"

Boone glared at him and pulled the rangers aside. "Isn't there something we can do?"

"Boone, you know the rules!" Jack whispered. "C'mon, man. If we let her in without a permit, we could lose our jobs. For heaven's sake, she could be fined big time, too, and your reputation will be shot. Do you want that?"

"Maybe we should let her in," Liz said. "It's *Boone.*"

"And that's precisely why I'm saying no!" Jack was adamant. "You want your business to fail like your old man's did? I know how hard this was for you to start back up again. I know what you've been through. Heck, we couldn't believe it when we heard you were back in action. Don't throw everything away for one girl."

But she was an important girl. Boone was more fond of her than he realized. He was looking forward to her company.

Boone looked at the blonde standing forlorn by herself. Where was this so-called date of hers? The guy was over there laughing like he didn't even care. That's not how you treat a woman. Anger grew like a raging fire.

"Well?" Parker skipped over to them. "What's the verdict? The bimbo can't go. *Right?*"

What? Hold your tongue, Boone! He tried to calm himself down before speaking.

"Don't call her that! Have some respect, man!"

"Whatever!"

"Kelly? Everyone? Can I have your attention?" Boone called the group over. Kelly shuffled behind, looking like she had been crying. "I'm so terribly sorry, Kelly. They won't let you in without a permit in your name, and it's too late to purchase one now, even if we could. It has to be done online, prior to arrival. I'm so sorry, sweetheart!"

Kelly burst into tears. She immediately shouted at Parker.

"You knew this would happen, *you jerk!* You're a lawyer for Pete's Sake! You knew it was in Sara's name! You knew it wasn't transferable! Give me my money back right now, you *stupid narc!*"

Parker threw his hands up and walked away. "You wanted to come!" He shouted back. His grandparents followed after him like two puppies.

Oh boy! Boone had a big problem now.

Lord help! I don't know what to do about this.

THE BETRAYAL

Boone left Kelly with Jack and Liz back at the beach. She was told she could walk along the shore, but only in clear sight. He couldn't help but feel like he let her down.

They were definitely taking that trip to Angoon after this. He would show Kelly his roots, especially since she said she was interested in Tlingit culture. There was plenty of that there.

He'd quickly take the other three to see the bears and then get back in the air. Boone didn't want to spend too much time with the Masons, especially since he couldn't stand their lawyer grandson. The grandparents were not as mobile as he'd hoped, so he knew they wouldn't be able to go far on foot.

Boone looked at his watch as they headed down the beach. He'd only take them to the viewing log. The grandparents had canes and moved like turtles. At this pace, they'd never get out of there.

Normally, his policy was to take anyone who could pay, but now Boone thought otherwise. If you can't walk properly, or you are a troublemaker, you can't go. Period. But how would he draft that? So often it came down to human rights. He was all for that, but this was not good. The grandparents were having a hard time. Their grandson wasn't even helping them. They lingered behind him.

Thankfully, they were just about at the viewing log, and that's as far as Boone was willing to take them under these conditions.

"We're here, folks," Boone announced to the group. "Take a seat on the log and wait for the bears to come to you."

"What do you mean, take a seat?" Parker complained. "I paid you good money to see some bears, and that's what we're doing!"

Boone pulled the lawyer aside and whispered, "Your grandparents can't make it much further. Are you going to carry them?"

Parker shook his head and pulled out his phone. He typed some notes into it and stuffed it back into his pocket. It looked like the guy was trying to intimidate him, but Boone wasn't having it. Let him try to sue him. That's what he pays the big bucks for. Insurance for this kind of business is not cheap for this very reason.

"Look... I'm sorry you're disappointed, but I'm the one in charge, and I call the shots," Boone went on. "Those two are a safety risk. I can't take them any further. What if one of them falls?"

"So!"

Figures he'd say that. "Just take a seat with your grandparents and enjoy the show. We'll be here for about two hours. If we're lucky, we might see a bear or two."

Parker stormed away and sat down beside his grandfather.

Boone was so frustrated. He knew he still had to go over the rules, but he was tired of the guy. Still, he had a job to do.

"Okay, everyone, listen up! We have a few rules to go over pertaining to the bear watch. I know the rangers already covered it, but I'm going to run them by you again, just to be sure we all stay safe."

"Please don't!"

Boone ignored the jerk.

"First rule. Stay at least 150 feet away from the bears at all times.

"What bears?" the guy complained again.

His grandparents shushed him before he could say anything more. At least he listened to them, *sort of.*

"No feeding the bears. No throwing things at them. Stay on the log, and keep your voices down.

Boone wasn't sure they'd get to see any bears today. It was mid-afternoon, and the best time to see them was morning and evening. Yet, it was mating season, so there should be plenty of them lurking around. It's better when the salmon spawn, but that was weeks away.

Second Chance Bear Guides doesn't guarantee a sighting. Bears are unpredictable, and that's not his fault. He made sure to tell them there was other wildlife to see besides bears.

"Look at the eagles," Boone pointed in the distance. He tried to drum up a conversation with the old guy, but he was pretty withdrawn. He just sat there stubbornly holding his cane.

"Look at the deer," the old lady pointed out, "I can see two of them towards the trees over there. Maybe a bear is after them. Chester, look!"

"I don't see no bear! Leave me alone!"

"Oh Chester-Pester, don't be so grumpy!"

The old man's wife tried to snuggle with him, but he wouldn't have it. Then she tickled him and he changed his attitude. The two of them hugged and doted on each other. It was heartwarming, and a total contrast to their grandson's bad behaviour.

Boone was told they were celebrating their 50th anniversary. A twinge of sorrow flooded in. Why didn't his parents last that long? He knew why. It was the alcohol and the cancer. He shook the memory as quickly as it came. This was not the time.

Just then, some ravens started croaking in a nearby spruce tree, pulling him out of his thoughts. At least someone was having fun.

The day was dragging on, and still no bears.

The couple sat with their canes in hand, waiting. Their grandson lay on the log, resting. At least he was quiet.

As time lingered, Boone decided to stretch his legs. He could feel sweat dripping down his red and black buffalo plaid shirt. His jeans stuck to him inside his hip waders as well. It was really getting warm. No wonder there were no bears. They were all snoozing in the sun.

Lord, can you bring me some bears?

Wincing in the sun, Boone decided to walk the perimeter,

scouting for bear scat. If it were fresh, he'd know they were around. If not, he knew it was a waste of time today.

Heading back early was not an option either. That was clear.

He'd keep the group in sight and head to the tree line. He'd go far enough to examine the ground, yet close enough to monitor the situation. No need to even tell them what he was doing.

While inside the tree line, all he could see was day-old scat. Nothing fresh. He saw traces of martins, but that was it.

Boone crouched down and sat at the base of an old deformed spruce. He rested his head against the scratchy bark, pausing to listen to nature. It was so calming and relaxing. He could spend all day there.

He wished the blonde had come. She would have made it much more interesting. She intrigued him. Especially because her faith was so brand new. It was a privilege to be the first person she told.

There was so much more to tell her. Hopefully, they could get going soon so he could fly them to Angoon. It would be a tight squeeze to get them there, but he'd done it before. Aunt Sally always had open arms. She'd give them supper and serve them her famous stink eggs and potatoes. They'd get a kick out of that, hopefully.

Boone decided he had better get moving before they figured out he was gone. He got up and suddenly heard a scream. It was the old lady. He took off in a hurry to the clearing, and there he saw it. The old man was too close to a bear.

What on earth?

Within minutes, Boone was back at the log. Parker and his grandmother were standing, calling the old man. They were also too close.

"What's going on? You guys all need to back up. Back up slowly!"

"Chester! Come back!"

The old man had a mind of his own. He was going even closer, hobbling with his cane. He kept looking back and inching forward. Was he crazy?

At this point, there was nothing Boone could do. He didn't have bear spray. To go closer to the grizzly without it would be stupid. Boone tried calling him back one more time! "Chester! Back up slowly!"

The old man shook his head in defiance.

His wife began to cry. "Chester, no! Not like this?"

What was going on here?

Then he heard Tweety asking her grandson for bear spray. What bear spray? Who had bear spray? Did Parker have some in his bag after all? He'd be mad later. Right now, he had to get it.

"Parker!" his grandmother cried, "Do something!"

Parker refused. He backed up with his bag in his hand, shaking his head, "No, I can't!"

Boone charged over to Parker and ripped away his backpack. Parker stumbled and fell on his butt. "I can't," he kept saying as he scooted backwards. "I can't!"

In a hurry, Boone rooted through the man's backpack and found the hidden bear spray. He'd have to use it fast.

Then, to the side, a smaller grizzly entered the clearing. A female. Would she get the male's attention? The large grizzly was heading right for Chester, just a few feet away. He stood on his hind legs.

The old man threw his cane at the bear.

Boone saw it set to charge, huffing and stomping. He ran as fast as he could to get there on time. Then, Boone pushed the old man out of the way and sprayed the grizzly.

The old man sat there and didn't move.

The bear roared and moved backward for a moment, then charged forward again. Boone looked at the old guy, inviting the bear. He had to get him away from it. Flapping his arms and yelling, he decided to try and get him to follow him instead. *Success!*

The bear charged toward Boone instead.

He stumbled and landed on his rear. Then, he aimed the bear spray one more time. With a gush to the face, the bear retreated. He meandered off toward the female, looking back and huffing.

That was close. *Too close!*

Boone felt his heart pounding in his chest. He breathed heavily, trying to catch his breath. One bad move and things could have gone sideways. If he hadn't had the bear spray, he'd be dead right now.

Thank you, Lord!

"ARE YOU OKAY?!" Tweety shrieked, extremely distraught. She cupped her mouth and sobbed. The woman wasn't just upset, she was also furious with her husband. She struck him with her cane, shouting profanities. Boone didn't know an old lady could swear like that.

He wanted to do the same. Instead, Boone composed himself and stood up. He dusted himself off and took a breath. "What were you thinking!?"

The old man just sat there and sobbed.

Boone knew. He wasn't dumb. He'd seen this kind of thing before. Not here, not like this, but it was definitely the same. Make no mistake.

This was suicide by bear.

THE CAT FIGHT

Kelly had taken a million pictures with her new camera since arriving at Pack Creek. There were so many more things to photograph than just bears on the island. She didn't think she'd see a bear where she was, but it was always a possibility. Ranger Liz told her there were over 1600 bears on the island. That kind of scared her.

"Just stay close to us. We have bear spray."

She didn't have a problem with that. Of course, she knew where she could and couldn't go. At first, she was angry that they wouldn't allow her in without a permit. But now, not so much.

It was a beautiful place. Something calmed her soul as she started walking around the shoreline. She had a nice chat with God. It was interesting that she kept feeling the need to have a conversation with Him. Then she remembered Boone's advice. *It's a relationship.*

Speaking of... Her relationship with Parker was over, if you could even call it that. It was a joke. All he had was charm and good looks. That's nothing if you don't have a heart!

Good riddance, she would tell him when he came back, whenever that would be. Boone told her two hours, but it had already been three. The day was waning.

Ranger Liz walked up beside her as a gust of wind blew. "Weather's changing."

"Ya think?"

"Yup! Might be sunny now, but trust me. Something's brewing. My mom calls me a human barometer."

Kelly laughed. The girl was sweet. She looked her age. She wore a brown Stetson hat with black braids down the side. Her uniform made her look important.

"Want one?" she handed her a pop. "We brought some in the cooler. Just make sure you give me the can. Pack it in, pack it out, you know."

"Sure!"

The two of them sat on a rock guzzling pop in the sun. It was nice. Kelly was out of her comfort zone, and she liked it. Nothing wrong with making new friends. It was hard at first, but this trip was a learning experience.

"Can I ask you something?" Liz asked her after belching like a man. Kelly was surprised something like that came out of her mouth.

"Excuse me!" Liz apologized for the burp. "So, how long have you known the pilot?"

Kelly looked at her sideways. She was after something.

"Oh, not long. I just met him today."

Liz spit out her pop and suddenly choked. "What? I mean... I've known Boone for a long time, and he doesn't normally freak out when someone can't go with him."

"What do you mean?"

"Girl, he's all over you!"

Kelly looked at her, stunned. "No! It's not like that."

"Well then, what is it like?"

Kelly didn't want to go into detail. She wasn't ready to share her Jesus moment, and the fact that she and Boone shared a common faith. "We talked on the plane, but that was it."

"Well, it must have been some conversation. It looks like you made quite the impression. I know Boone, and he's a tough nut to crack. He's all wild and charming on the outside, but inside, nobody can touch that."

"So, you two were a thing?"

"Not were, ARE!"

And there it was. If there was one thing Kelly could do well, it was read between the lines. What the girl was really trying to say was, Get your hands off my man. That's probably the only reason she came over.

Kelly couldn't blame her. Boone was quite attractive. His

flaming red hair was mesmerizing. His blue eyes had a way of looking right into your soul. And his kind personality was heartwarming. The man was fine indeed.

"Look, I'm not after your boyfriend. I just met him. We had a conversation, that's all."

The girl looked smug. "That's how they all start, honey. Boone and I have been together since high school. We lived together before he went to prison."

"Prison?"

Maybe Boone wasn't who she thought he was.

"Yup. He screwed up big time."

Kelly knew why she was telling her this. The girl was trying to scare her away. Why would she be airing his dirty laundry if she was in love with the man? Ted played these games with her, and they weren't nice.

"Well, we all make mistakes."

"Not like this, you don't! Aren't you going to ask me what he did?"

"Nope!" Kelly said point-blank, refusing to play her game.

Suddenly, Liz's walkie-talkie squawked. "Liz, you there? It's Boone. Over."

"See, my honey's calling me now. Yeah, what's up sunshine? Over." She winked at Kelly as if to prove her point.

"We had a bear scare. Can you and Jack come with the stretcher? We've got a man down. Over."

Kelly's eyes grew wide. She wondered who it was. Was it Parker? He may be a jerk, but he didn't deserve this. Was it Tweety, or maybe Chester? She had to know!"

"Copy that. Do you need the wheeled or the basket litter? Over?"

"Wheeled. Over."

"Let me talk to him, please!" Kelly insisted, reaching for the walkie-talkie. "I gotta find out what happened. Are they okay?"

"You think I'm nuts? I'm not letting you talk to him. This is my job. We're the professionals here. You're just... Well, you know!"

The girl showed her true colours now. How could she be so cruel?

Liz notified Jack through the walkie-talkie and said she'd be right there. Kelly didn't know what she was supposed to do. Maybe they would let her in now? After all, she was a nurse's aide. Surely there was something she could help with.

"I can help! I know first aid and CPR."

"So do I, honey. Besides, you are not allowed in, remember? Just go back to the plane and wait for us there. It's the safest place to be. Heaven forbid a bear comes along when we're not here to protect you. Whatever will you do?"

Kelly ignored the barb and stood helpless as the two rangers joined up. One rolled a stretcher and the other helped push it.

"Remember what I said," Liz shouted as they took off toward the trail.

Suddenly, loneliness crept back in. Kelly looked around and felt a chill. Maybe she should go back to the plane like Liz said.

All she had to do was wade through the water again. It wasn't far, yet the water was deeper than when they first arrived.

She rolled up her pant legs, took off her hiking boots and socks, and stuffed them in her bag. With a sigh, she did what she was told, hoping it wouldn't be too long before they were back.

God Almighty, please take care of them!

RESCUE ME

By the time both rangers got to the viewing log, Tweety managed to get Chester on his feet. Up until then, he sat inconsolable in the grassy meadow where the attack took place. He refused to budge.

It didn't matter what he said to the old guy. He wouldn't respond. At first, Boone thought he was in shock, but this was no shock. The old guy had a death wish, like he assumed.

He found out from his wife that Chester had stage four terminal colon cancer. That's why his stomach was so large. She said they didn't even have time to treat it. He got sick only six months ago with a little stomach bug that wouldn't go away.

Poor man.

Boone understood his desperation, but going out by grizzly was not the way to go either. Uncle Pete passed away from lung cancer and refused treatment. What he went through in the end was barbaric. He could understand not wanting to die that way.

Tweety told him Chester used to work in the zoo when they met. He was responsible for the bear sanctuary, so he was familiar with their behaviour. The old man had a dream to go to Alaska one last time and see them in the wild. Boone was told Parker had tried to get him into other bear guides, but nobody would take him because of his knees, obesity, and age. Second Chance Bear Guides was the only one without medical qualifications.

Boone made a mental note to draft a new policy as soon as he gets home. As hard as it was, he'd have to screen his customers. They will have to meet certain physical and mental criteria from now on. He'd have to meet with a lawyer when he gets back, even if it means a hefty bill.

For a moment, Boone thought of asking Parker for legal advice, but then realized that would be stupid. He had no desire to do business with the guy. Granted, he owed him his life because of the bear spray, but the fact that he lied about it and said he didn't have any in his bag still ticked him off.

And what was the man doing now? Obsessing over his dirty shoes? Who cares how expensive they are?

Of all the things to worry about right now, shoes were not one of them. He didn't even bother to console his grandfather. It was like he didn't even care.

"Let's go!" Parker complained. "This mud has ruined my Oxfords. You're paying for them, *Boone!* If that's even your real name!"

Boone just ignored him. There were more important things to attend to.

"He doesn't know any better, you know," the grandmother whispered. "He's had a hard life, my Parker. He was adopted when he was eight years old. Came from a rough life. My daughter did the best she could, but he never fit in. Her ex didn't want anything to do with him, so we helped raise him. Put him through law school and everything, but he's still... *not right.*"

You can say that again!

Boone felt sorry for the man. His grandiose behaviour was alarming, but it pointed to a deeper problem: His soul. There was something terribly wrong with him.

Boone had seen all kinds in prison. Many were broken men like Parker who had reinvented themselves to deal with the pain. It was like they killed off the old version of themselves and replaced it with a monster. Yet, the trauma was still there, hidden deep in the soul where he knew only Jesus could find it and heal it. It was painful to see, and he was glad he escaped that life before it destroyed him completely.

Thoughts of his buddy, Jimmy, came to mind. He was still there.

My God! Please help him!

Boone assisted the rangers as they helped Chester get into

the stretcher. He went kicking and screaming, claiming it was completely unnecessary. It was just in case. He was in his eighties with bad knees. His cancer was an issue, as well as his mental state. He was going to take a ride whether he wanted to or not.

It was late afternoon already. He'd have to skip the trip to Angoon and take the old man back to Juneau instead. He'd need a mental health assessment at the hospital, as well as a medical check. Though he couldn't prove the man's motives for provoking the bear, it was worth mentioning to the doctor.

Boone wondered if he should even bother. The guy was on his last legs. If he made a big deal out of it, they wouldn't be able to finish the cruise. It might do more harm than good.

He'd have a chat with the rangers about it once they got back to the station.

As they neared the shoreline, Boone could see his plane floating in the water where he had left it. He was thankful Liz told Kelly to go wait in there. That's why he always keeps it unlocked. Things happen in the wilderness. The plane was the safest place to be, considering the circumstances.

Once they arrived at the ranger station, Jack and Liz assessed the old man once more, making sure he was fit to go. Boone talked to them privately, getting their take on the situation.

"So, you think I should just do nothing?" Boone whispered with the rangers while the old couple and their grandson stood at the door, eager to leave.

"I would!" Liz spoke up.

That said it all. Boone knew not to trust her with ethics. He'd been burned by her before. Memories of their old relationship flooded his mind. *That's over, bud! Move on!*

"Let's just discuss it with them," Boone asked him as he walked over to the door. "Do you want to go to the hospital or not, Mr. Mason?"

"No way!" Chester barked. "I told you no, the first time! I'm fine! Just a little shaken up. Besides, you promised us Angoon!"

That he did. Boone sighed, not knowing what to do.

"And you? Mrs. Mason? What do you want to do?"

The old woman teared up and looked at her husband. They locked their arms together and kissed. "No hospital! Let's just go to Angoon!"

"All right then," Boone said, thinking this was nuts, "I guess we're flying to Angoon. You alright with this, Parker?"

Tweety elbowed her grandson, who looked up from playing on his phone.

"Hugh? What?"

"Are you okay with going to Angoon?"

"Yah, whatever. You know there's no service here, right?"

Boone shook his head. The guy was a fool. He could use him, though. He'd have to borrow a few things from the rangers for the trip. The stuff Nate and Liam forgot. He'd also need to check the cargo hold for all the necessary emergency gear and make sure it was all there. He should have done it earlier, but unfortunately, he'd have to live it down.

"I know there's no service," Boone mused. "So...Parker, you can stay here with me. I need your help to get some supplies if we're going to fly to Angoon. Liz will take Mr. and Mrs. Mason to the plane. She's going to take you guys in the dinghy because of the high tide. I hope that's okay."

They nodded and headed out with Liz.

Thankfully, his Cessna had only burned about seven gallons of fuel so far. He had more than enough to make it to Angoon. Even back to Juneau. But he'd fuel up in Angoon just to be safe.

If they wanted to go to Angoon, they were going to Angoon. He'd radio Aunt Sally that they'd be coming for supper. Her sourdough bread was the best in Alaska. He couldn't wait!

Maybe this would get him a five-star review after all. Hopefully, it wasn't too late. He'd have to try and smooth things over with Parker first.

"Let's go get the gear!"

"Right!" Parker stopped fiddling with his phone and followed the redheaded lumberjack. "Hey, just to let you know, I-

I deliberately didn't use the bear spray back there. I wanted you to use it because… well, you know, you're the expert. Like, that's the story we're going with. Go it?"

Yeah, I got it, buddy!

THE RIGHT ONE

Kelly could see the old couple and the ranger coming in the dinghy. From the look of them, they seemed fine. Who was hurt then? Parker?

Oh Lord!

When they approached the plane, she flung open the door, not wasting any time at all. "Are you okay?"

"We're fine, dear!" Tweety shouted over the dinghy motor, "Just some bumps and bruises."

Liz threw her a rope, and she eased them in. The two of them helped Chester and Tweetie into the cabin of the plane without saying much. It was only after Liz left, and they were safe in the cabin of the plane, that Chester started sobbing.

"I know, I know, dear!" his wife consoled him.

"What happened?"

"Oh, honey, you don't want to know."

"Yes, I do! Is Parker hurt? What about Boone?"

Tweety filled her in on every detail. It sounded terrible: The bear charging. Boone's narrow escape. She was glad she wasn't there after all. Yet, some things didn't add up.

Kelly knew seniors. She made a living taking care of their every need. She knew something was up and decided to confront them like she did at work. Sometimes, the only way to deal with them was to be blunt.

"Chester? Did you want to die?"

Chester immediately burst into tears. She had her answer.

"How long do you have?"

Tweety sobbed, "They said three months. He has colon cancer."

"I can do my own talking," he sniffed and tried to compose

himself. "I don't want to die from some embarrassing bum disease. I want to go out in a blaze of glory. *I miss the bears.* I miss being young. My body doesn't work no more. I'm sorry."

Tweety hung her head. "You should have said something to me, Chester."

"You would have stopped me!"

"Darn right I would have! Did Parker know?"

Silence.

That would be a yes.

Kelly couldn't understand why their own grandson would consent to something as stupid as this. She was not in favour of euthanasia nor anything that resembled it. She'd address that later, though. Right now, there was only one thing left to do. *Pray!*

"I'm going to tell you guys something. I'm kind of new at this, so please be patient," Kelly swallowed hard. She wasn't used to expressing herself like this. "I-I found Jesus."

Chester and Tweety listened.

"You see, I know what it's like to be lost. I was lost in *here,*" she pointed to her heart. "I let everyone and everything dictate to me how my life should go. After a while, I didn't even know who I was anymore. I could be standing in a crowd and feel invisible. I could be visiting someone, or at work, and feel so lonely I could barely cope."

Kelly tried to find the words so they made sense. She felt like she had marbles in her mouth. Why wouldn't the words come out right?

"What I'm trying to say is... I just decided to talk to God, and I was shocked that he answered me. It wasn't in an audible way. I'm not nuts or anything. It was in my heart. I just felt better. Like, better than I've ever felt before. I want you to have that same peace, Chester."

Chester began to sob.

"We go to church, right, Chester? We know about the

Eucharist and Holy Communion, as well as the Sacraments. We already know about Mary's son, Jesus, on the cross. We go to confession. We attend mass every week. Isn't that the same thing?"

"I'm not talking about church or even a specific kind of church. You see, my Nana told me all about Jesus when I was growing up. I knew all the head knowledge about how to be a believer, but it was just information. You need a heart connection."

Tweety looked confused.

"Just trust me on this, guys. What I'm trying to say is you have to talk to God. It's about a relationship, not information. Receiving Jesus is a choice. You just choose to believe. You communicate with him."

"Honey, we know you mean well, but if you're trying to say all we need to do is pray and all our problems will suddenly disappear, you're barking up the wrong tree. It doesn't work like that. There's a long list of things you need to do first before you can call yourself a Catholic. It's not that easy."

Kelly wanted to say, *It IS that easy!* It wasn't about being Catholic, or Jewish, or protestant, or any other faith. It was about a relationship with Jesus Christ.

She couldn't get them to understand. Clearly, they thought they knew more than her. Maybe they did. Maybe they were talking about two different things. It definitely didn't sound like what she and Boone were talking about earlier. All she knew was how she felt. Even now, she could feel God tugging at her heart to stop. *Why God?*

Maybe not everyone was capable of understanding. Maybe it was the way she was coming across. After all, what did she know about evangelism? As Boone told her so eloquently, she was just a baby Christian.

"Okay, well... I just thought praying would help Chester."

"Thank you, my dear!" Chester sniffed, "I appreciate it. We can pray if you like. I just don't have a prayer book with me. Tweety? Do you know any prayers off by heart?"

Now Kelly was confused. *What on earth?* This wasn't at all what she was expecting. Why didn't they understand how easy it was?

"I can pray. No worries," Kelly told them. They all bowed their heads as she prayed for Jesus to comfort Chester through his sickness and give him hope to carry on.

Her heart broke that they didn't understand. Her heart broke that they didn't seem to have or even want a heart connection. Under her breath, she prayed one more thing. *Jesus, help them to know how simple your love is. Help them to understand that they can have a personal relationship with you, without having to earn it. Help them know that your perfect peace is available to them, just like it was available to me.*

Like Boone said, all you have to do is believe. It's a free gift... but you have to actually want it.

Why wouldn't you want it?

Kelly watched the two of them try to comfort each other, yet they refused the greatest comforter of all time. *Jesus.*

Maybe they were talking about a totally different Jesus.

Thank the Lord, I know the right one!

KELLS-BELLS

Once the plane was packed up and everyone was in their seats, Boone brought the Cessna 180 to life again. They taxied away from shore and headed into the blue horizon. Below, they could see humpback whales tossing their bodies into the air, and harbour seals gathered in haul-out sites along the rocky cliffside.

"Look, everyone!" Boone pointed below, "Do you see them?"

The group pressed their faces against the windows. Everyone seemed enamoured by the marine life. It was, indeed, spectacular.

Boone observed the group as well. They seemed fine. It was almost as if nothing had happened at all. In fact, nothing really did happen, thank the Lord. It was just him. He was the one who almost got mauled by a grizzly bear.

Chester was foolish and could have gotten mauled as well, but thankfully Boone caught the bear's attention in time. The old man didn't know how close he came to being that bear's lunch.

Shivers crept up his spine with the thought of it. Boone had some close encounters before, but never that close. That was downright ugly. He still reeled over it.

Thank you, Lord, for sparing us!

Boone's stomach rumbled. It was time for supper. He could hardly wait to eat Aunt Sally's meal. It was always a highlight whenever he visited Angoon.

She was such a gracious host. They had an agreement that whenever he brought guests, he'd toss a couple of hundred bucks her way. He should make her and the boys official employees when he gets back. Write up the whole deal properly.

"Hey, Kelly-Bells," he called the blonde, hoping he wasn't

being too forward with the nickname. "Why don't you come up front?"

He was getting a little lonely.

Blushing, she popped her head up and unbuckled her seatbelt. He really enjoyed her company. He also wanted a chance to apologize for what happened with the permit situation.

"I hope the nickname is okay," Boone smirked. "I'm sure you heard that one before."

"Yes, a million times, but that's okay."

Boone could see she had something on her mind. She had the type of face you could read like a book. He liked reading that book. "What's up?"

The girl bit her lip and looked back at the others.

"Don't worry," he switched the headsets to private talk. "He can't hear us. Like before."

"Oh, no... that's not it," she said. "That ship has sailed! I don't want to have anything more to do with the guy. Seriously! Need I say more?"

"Nope!" Boone burst out laughing.

"Don't laugh. That was a hard lesson!"

Boone tried not to be so enthusiastic. It was comical. He saw this coming, yet he felt bad for her. "It happens to the best of us."

"Yah, mostly me."

He couldn't help but laugh again. "Sorry."

Boone sure loved her smile. Mysterious, yet innocent. Why did he love talking to her so much? It was a pleasant distraction from this nasty trip. Like sunshine in the rain.

"Look, I just wanted to apologize again about the permit situation. I should have caught it before we left. Usually, I check IDs before the flight. I was in a hurry and I missed a step. I could have prevented this."

"It wasn't your fault."

"Yah, it was."

The two of them chuckled. He was an idiot. *You like the girl, so ask her out.* Boone didn't want to listen to his conscience.

He'd made too many mistakes with women to trust his own judgment, yet something told him to try.

"Let me make it up to you," he said before he realized what was coming out of his mouth. "Let me take you on a date."

Kelly sat there with a wide grin. "Oh, I see."

"What's that supposed to mean?"

"Well, your girlfriend Liz might not be so happy about that."

"What?" Boone gasped, "She's not my girlfriend!"

"That's not what she says. She told me all about you."

Boone couldn't tell if she was teasing him or not. He couldn't believe Liz's big mouth. Or, rather, he could. He knew what she was like. They ended things a long time ago.

"What did she say?"

"I'll spare you the details. I'm not that naive. I knew what she was up to the moment she opened her mouth. She was all territorial and everything. Basically, she told me, Hands off her guy!"

Boone's eyes went wide. He couldn't believe Liz still had a thing for him. He couldn't believe she would stoop this low. There was definitely nothing between them anymore.

"I'm sorry you had to go through that. That's brutal!"

"Tell me about it!"

They both laughed at the same time. Boone decided to make one more attempt at asking her out. This time she said yes. Once they got back, he would take her up the Tram. The Sunshine Liner had a rare double-day stay in Juneau, and he was taking full advantage of it. He had no more tours booked anyway, and he definitely needed a day off after this.

"Anyway, I asked you what was on your mind earlier," Boone changed the subject. "Care to elaborate?"

Kelly looked serious. She explained what happened with the Masons and how she botched her attempt to evangelize them. He was just about to answer her when he noticed the clouds. They were getting thicker. His Doppler showed a storm right in front of them. He should have been paying more attention instead of flirting with Kelly.

Stupid!

"Everyone! Can I have your attention?" he said, turning his headset back so everyone could hear. Boone realized he was waking them up, but this was important.

Kelly sat up straight and looked alarmed.

"Looks like we have some bad weather ahead of us. I'll try to go around, but it might get a little bumpy. Make sure your seat belts are tight!"

Boone eyed the skies. The dark clouds came in quickly. He'd try to find a way around, but the rain started pounding them. Thunder cracked hard amongst the lightning.

"Should I go back to my seat?" Kelly asked him.

Suddenly, a flash of lightning hit the wing, knocking them around.

"Um," Boone tried to concentrate on his gauges. They were going crazy. "Stay where you are!"

The turbulence was unreal. They bounced around uncontrollably. Boone could barely hold the plane steady.

"Anything I can do?"

"Yeah, you can be my second set of eyes. Let me know what you see and when you see it. Visibility is not great. I also have copilot controls just in case something happens."

Boone quickly explained how the copilot controls work. He hoped he didn't need them.

"Everyone, get your life preservers on! They're under your seats. And remember what I said. Do not inflate them!"

"Kelly! Get yours on! It's under your seat!"

"What about you?"

"I'll get mine on later. Right now, I need my hands!"

Suddenly, a large crack of thunder shook the plane hard. The storm tossed them to and fro. Boone tried to steady it, but he was losing control.

"Look, I see water. Can we land?"

"Maybe."

Then, lightning hit them hard again. He knew right then that they were going down. "I guess we have no choice now."

The passengers in the back screamed.

"MAYDAY! MAYDAY! MAYDAY! This is November Five Eight Zero Delta Bravo, Cessna 180. We are going down!"

Lightning hit again. Winds howled. Thunder cracked. Rain pelted the windshield. Boone couldn't see the water below. He aimed for the bay as best he could. He hoped the pontoons could withstand the impact.

Suddenly, they hit hard! The plane shook violently as it rumbled too fast over the turbulent water. *I can't hold it!* Everything was vibrating. He could feel the flip coming. Then a *Boom!* They were upside down!

Water filled the fuselage.

GETTING OUT

Kelly was underwater. She remembered what Boone said. Inflate after you clear the wreckage, but she was still trapped inside.

Lights flashed on and off.

I must get to them. Chester and Tweety hung upside down from their seatbelts. She swam to release them.

Where was Parker?

Where was Boone?

Could she hold her breath for longer? She tugged at the old couple's seat belts until they released. Their lifeless bodies fell toward her as she moved them through the door.

Rise! Rise!

The torrential rains peppered her face as she popped above water. It was dark and stormy with waters raging. She pulled the toggle at the front of her life jacket, and it quickly inflated.

Chester popped to the surface first, then Tweety. She swam to them and pulled their toggles as well. Tweety came to, screaming for her husband. Chester wasn't moving.

The thunder was too loud. The rain pummelled her face, and it was hard to see. Kelly shouted as hard as she could. "*Boone! Parker!*"

They weren't rising to the surface! Where were they? Could they still be trapped inside? Should she go back down?

Then suddenly, Parker's head popped up right next to her. He was conscious. He didn't have a life preserver on, and he was flailing his arms like he was drowning. "Where's your life jacket?"

He was terrified. He tried to dunk her. "*No, Parker, stop!*" Again, he was using her to stay afloat.

Kelly sank underwater, then came back up again, bobbing up and down with every attempt Parker made to save himself. He was drowning her. *"Stop!"*

Then, out of nowhere, Boone appeared, dragging a vest. He tried to rip Parker off her. It didn't work.

Again, he held her head under water. Panic. She couldn't breathe. The water was choking her. Or were Parker's hands around her neck? She couldn't tell. She couldn't stay above water.

Then again, Boone tried to rip Parker off her. He punched him in the face until he stopped and fell limp. "Moron!" she heard Boone say.

Blurry-eyed, Kelly gasped for air, finally getting free of his clutches. She pushed herself away from both men and wiped her eyes. It was still raining hard, but she could finally see what was happening.

Boone was putting a life jacket on Parker. He got it on his unconscious body and pulled the toggle to inflate it. "That's all you had to do, buddy!"

"Thank you!"

"Here! Grab the rope!" Boone told her.

Kelly grabbed hold as he pulled her to him. He tied it to her and Parker and did the same with Tweety and Chester.

They all huddled together as a group, bobbing in the treacherous water. Rain continued to pelt them, and thunder and lightning flashed around them. The half-submerged plane banged around a few feet away. Only one pontoon floated beside them.

The plane was quickly going under.

"We need to get to shore!" Boone shouted, "Can you swim?"

Kelly nodded, "But Chester's hurt!" She saw that his head was bleeding and he was unconscious. Tweety was screaming his name.

"Chester!" Boone shook him, "Chester!" He felt for a pulse, then shook his head, telling her what she didn't want to hear.

No, it couldn't be! She would check herself.

CPR! They could do CPR. She was trained. She was a strong swimmer. She knew how to do mouth-to-mouth. All they had to do was get him to shore.

But there was no pulse.

Kelly checked again. She checked his wrist. She checked his neck. There was no pulse. Finally, she checked his head wound and realized there was no surviving *that*.

He's gone!

Tweety was still frantic. She wouldn't stop screaming. She must think he's still alive. "Chester!!"

God, help us!

After a while, the violent storm started to subside, but the current in the lake was still very strong. It would take a lot of strength to fight it to shore with Chester as part of the group.

It was either him or them.

Kelly looked at Boone, and they both realized what must be done. They tied unconscious Parker together with his grandmother and removed the rope from Chester. Boone took off the man's lifejacket.

He slowly sank below the surface.

The two of them turned back to Parker and Tweety. He had regained consciousness and was shaking his grandmother. "Something is wrong with her!"

Boone quickly assessed her. "Tweety! Tweety!!" He shook her, then felt for a pulse. There was nothing more he could do. He shook his head to let her know she passed.

NO!

She was just alive a minute ago! "Tweety!!" Kelly felt for a pulse. She felt her neck. She felt her wrist. There was no breathing. It was apparent. She was gone, too.

"NO!" Kelly screamed.

Her heart must have given out. This was too much for her! It was hard enough for a young person. The current was sucking them under. What kind of lake was this?

Boone untied the rope from Tweety and removed her life jacket like he did her husband. There was no other way.

She slowly sank under the water.

"We gotta get out of here! The current is too strong!" Boone shouted. "Parker, can you swim?"

"Yah!" he said, wiping his face.

With rope in tow, the three of them swam against the current. It was useless. They were going nowhere.

"Kick hard!" Boone told them both, "It's got a strong tidal current. It must be Kootznahoo Inlet, one of the worst lakes.

The freezing cold water was an incredible danger as well. Kelly knew they only had minutes before hypothermia set in. She kicked hard. They all kicked hard.

Then... there it was. She could feel the bottom.

All three of them dragged their soaking bodies through the muck. They pushed through the reeds. They fought against the rain, which was only light now. Thunder rolled in the distance as they reached the water's edge. They were out.

They were out!

Kelly dropped to her knees on the sand and cried, "THANK YOU, JESUS! THANK YOU!"

Boone removed his lifejacket and told her to remove hers as well. Parker already had his off. "We have to get warm, fast!"

Kelly knew why.

"I have some waterproof matches I always carry. Can you guys find some twigs and moss? Maybe under some trees. Something that didn't get wet from the rain."

"Look, Boone!" Kelly pointed, "floating in the water. Two of your totes. I'm going to go get them."

"Be careful!"

Two totes washed ashore near the tree line just south of where they came in. Kelly ran to get them and dragged them over to the men. One had emergency supplies like a flare gun, rope, flashlights, newspaper, matches, lighter fluid, and jackets. The other one had food, water bottles and blankets. It was an answer to her prayers.

"No satellite phone?" Boone asked.

"I don't see anything else in the tote."

"Great! It was supposed to be with the flare gun. The boys must have forgotten to grab it from my desk! I was charging the battery the night before we left. Darn!"

Parker came back with an armful of branches and dropped them in place. He must have overheard the conversation.

"You are the worst! This is your fault! IT'S ALL YOUR FAULT! Now what am I supposed to do?"

"We're all in the same boat, buddy! Just try to calm down."

"Calm down? Don't tell me to calm down! What a joke! Your Mickey Mouse business cost me my grandparents' lives! You're gonna pay for this, you idiot!"

"I'm sorry, okay. I didn't mean for any of this to happen. I'm sorry we lost them. *I'm sorry!*"

Boone walked in one direction, Parker in another. The two of them just had to cool off. She would make the fire. She would make the campsite cozy. She would do everything, just like she always did.

Then everything would be okay.

CREEP

The flames jumped high and spat into the midnight air as Kelly added another log to the fire. The two men came back hours ago and helped her set up camp.

At least Boone did. Parker just sat there.

They shivered, still damp from the lake. At least there were enough dry blankets and jackets for everyone. Kelly could feel herself slowly warming up. That was a good thing. She didn't think her teeth would ever stop chattering.

Boone tied a rope around the campsite to form a perimeter to prevent unwanted bear encounters. She hoped it would help. He positioned a flashlight at each corner so they could see the specific area.

Their beachfront campsite butt up against the water's edge. The hope was to stay visible so search and rescue could find them. Boone seemed certain his aunt would send help when they didn't show up in Angoon.

"So, where do you figure we are?"

Boone scooted over to her. He draped his blanket around her shivering shoulders. "Well... as far as I can tell, we're somewhere in Kootznahoo Inlet, the eastern shore of Chatham Strait."

Parker sat by himself, glaring at the two of them. She noticed his demeanour had changed. He was upset before, for good reason, but now, something seemed off with him.

"You okay, Parker?" she asked.

"Don't pretend you care!"

"Dude! Stop!" Boone insisted. "Not again!"

She hoped the two men would be civil, at least until they were rescued. She was right in the middle of this, whatever this was. Sure, he lost his grandparents, and that must be devastating, but why the constant bickering? It wasn't helping their situation.

From the flicker of the campfire, she could see the dark circles under Parker's eyes. Had he taken a blow to the head? Had they missed that? Should she check? She was the healthcare professional.

Parker got up and walked away before she could say anything.

"Anyway," Boone continued, "I hope my Aunt Sally called Angoon search and rescue by now. When I say I'll be somewhere, I keep my word. She knows that."

"Maybe it's too stormy for them right now? It could've moved away from us and over to them."

"Maybe."

Parker came back with a whole handful of protein bars for himself. He was already stuffing one of them into his mouth.

"Dude, that's all we got!" Boone told him. "Maybe try sharing."

Parker ignored him and made a point of chewing noisily, with his mouth wide open like a pig. It was as if he were taunting Boone.

The man stood there and laughed like he was insane. Then he roared, pretending he was a bear or something. He ripped a piece of a protein bar with his teeth aggressively.

What the heck is this guy's problem?

Then, she saw his face again. Did he smear mud under his eyes? Or, did he really have bruises? It was her duty to find out. He could be seriously injured.

"Parker? Are you hurt?" she asked. "Let me see your eyes, they're all bruised up!"

"Kelly, don't!" Boone warned.

Before she knew it, Parker had her in a chokehold. He dragged her backward and shouted, "GET BACK!"

Kelly couldn't breathe. He was cutting off her air supply. She tried to pull his arm away, but he was too strong.

"Okay, okay! Boone tried to reason, "Just let her go!"

"NO! SHE'S MINE!"

Kelly couldn't even scream. Only muffles and squeaks came out of her mouth. Tears ran down her face. Her throat hurt! All she could do was look at Boone in terror. *HELP ME!*

"Look! Whatever you have against me, it has nothing to do with her. LET HER GO!"

"NO!" Parker pulled out the flare gun and threatened him with it. "I'll use it! "Don't think I won't!"

"WHOA! Okay, okay! I'm backing up. You can have her! You can have her, I said!"

Kelly's eyes went wide. What was happening?

Parker dragged her backward away from the fire. She kicked and screamed and tried to bite him. Nothing released her from his clutches. It was hopeless.

He dragged her beyond the perimeter Boone had set up. It was dark. They were in the tree line. What was going to happen now? Where was Boone? She couldn't see him. He had abandoned her.

He had abandoned her.

Lord! ME!

Parker threw her down to the ground like a wild animal. He unbuckled his belt and unzipped his pants. He went charging for her, but she scooted backward on her bum into the bushes.

"Get away from me, you creep!"

Then, suddenly, from behind, Boone jumped him. They both fell to the ground. The two of them pummelled each other with their fists, over and over. One took a slug, then the other.

They fought inches away from Kelly. What could she do? How could she stop this? *Who would win?*

Where was the flare gun? *Over there!*

Could she get to it? Kelly tried to scoot toward it, but they were in the way. Parker slugged Boone in the jaw. Then Boone hit back hard. Back and forth, they wrestled and grunted.

Finally, Boone pinned him down. He took a swing at the man's jaw, over and over. Again. Over and over. Parker suddenly went limp.

Boone was sitting on top of him. He was the victor. He had taken Parker over by force. He had won.

But Boone couldn't stop.

Over and over, he hit Parker's head. One side, then the other. Again. Boone plowed his fist into his skull. Over and over. Again and again.

Parker didn't move.

"Boone, stop!"

He didn't hear her. "Stop!" Kelly cried, "STOP!"

Huffing and puffing, Boone finally stopped the assault. He sat on the motionless man and tried to catch his breath. "Give me the rope!"

"The rope?"

"Over there!" Boone motioned to the ground. He still had the man pinned, even though he wasn't moving.

She threw him the rope, and he quickly tied the man's hands together. Then he tied his feet. "There! He ain't going nowhere!"

Parker still lay motionless.

"Is he dead?"

"No!" Boone huffed, "But he should be!"

The two of them dragged his unconscious body back to the fire, placed him on his back, and used one of the blankets to keep him warm. His face was all bloody. Boone beat him up pretty good.

The two of them finally sat down by the fire, Boone in obvious pain. He draped a blanket over both their shoulders and pulled her to his chest. She leaned her head into him, and she suddenly burst out sobbing.

"I know, sweetie, I know!"

THE FOG

The sun came up early with the sound of ravens croaking in the distance. Boone walked as far as he dared to relieve himself. The fog that drifted in overnight made them vulnerable to a bear attack.

He'd have to keep his eyes peeled.

Boone wondered how long it would take to rescue them. He hadn't told anyone, but lightning took out the plane's navigation and GPS. That made finding them even more difficult. He wondered if he should try going for help.

Leaving Kelly behind was not an option. Leaving the creep alone with her was not an option. *What do I do, Lord?*

Boone knew he had lost control. He gave Parker a severe beating. He made sure he was breathing, but he wasn't exactly sure he was going to be okay. It all depended on how thick his skull was.

Boone figured, pretty thick.

His own head throbbed from the beating Parker gave him. The man had quite a punch. Boone touched his sore jaw and winced. His lip was split, and his beard was sticky with dry blood, but he would survive.

Suddenly, Kelly yelled for him to come. "Boone, he's awake!"

Boone ran to see. The man was sitting up; that was a good sign. He'd give him a piece of his mind now, and he was not untying him.

"So, what do you gotta say for yourself? Hugh?" Boone kicked the creep's foot as he walked by. "Bet your head hurts just about as bad as mine does."

Kelly watched from a distance.

"I-I don't know what got into me."

"I do!"

The man's face was pretty bruised, but the bleeding looked like it had stopped. His eyes weren't crossed, so Boone figured he would survive. He'd seen plenty of these beatings in prison. He knew who would make it and who wouldn't.

Boone knelt beside the man and whispered, "You EVER touch her again, and I'll kill you!"

Parker didn't say a word. He just shrugged and sat there looking at him with a blank stare. Boone was glad because he didn't think he could hold himself back if he opened his big mouth again.

"Hey, Kells?" Boone turned on a dime, "Let's get some grub!"

The two of them got the fire going. They dragged the food tote closer to them and started rummaging through it. It had spent the night away from camp. Boone knew it was safer for them. Bears had good noses.

They opened sardine cans, salmon, and tuna cans, and guzzled bottled water. Parker had eaten all the protein bars already. All that was left were some apples, oranges, and a bag of mixed fresh vegetables.

"Sorry, I can't offer you something better. I wish I had some bread."

"Oh, I couldn't eat it anyway. I'm gluten-free."

"Bah!" Parker laughed so hard, "that's what she did to me the other night. Now, it's your turn, buddy. She's a total loon! She can't even eat normal food!"

"Hey!" Boone reminded him, "what did I say? Shut your big mouth or I'll shut it for you!"

Kelly looked forlorn. She shook her head and apologized. "I-I have a medical condition. I can't help it. Ever heard of Celiac?"

"Yup! My dad had it. I carry the genes, too, but they're not active."

Kelly's mouth hung open.

"It's common in redheads. You're not from Scotland, are you?" he chuckled.

"No!" Kelly laughed, "I can't believe you know about this."

"Yah! My dad struggled with it. They even connect it to addictions and mental illness. All kinds of stuff. Dad refused to go gluten-free. It didn't end well."

"I'm sorry."

"My neighbour cooks me gluten-free perogies, and my Aunt Sally makes a great gluten-free sourdough bread. Her whole house is gluten-free just for me. She's the one who told me to be proactive so my genes don't turn on. Believe me, I do not want to end up like my father."

"Oh, you have daddy issues, too, I see. Looks like we have something else in common."

"Do tell!"

"Seriously?" Parker interrupted, "Maybe stop flirting right in front of me, why don't you! *Sheesh!*"

Was the guy picking a fight again? This was unreal. Didn't he learn his lesson the first time? "Stop it, NOW!" he held up a fist to warn him.

"Ooo big man!"

"That's it!" Boone stomped over there. "You want me to put a gag in it? I will! Or maybe my foot. Hugh? How would you like that?"

"Boone, stop!" Kelly insisted.

Parker began to laugh. "She still wants me!"

It was bad enough that he pushed his buttons, but to harass Kelly like that was unacceptable. "Take it back!"

"No!"

"Stop it, you guys! I can't take this anymore!" Kelly stormed off.

Great! Now what was he supposed to do? First, she wanted him to defend her; now she didn't. Why would she tell him to stop? Surely she didn't still have feelings for the guy.

"Kelly, wait!"

Suddenly, a Bible verse hit him hard. It was one he had memorized from prison. He knew God was telling him something, but he didn't want to listen, not now.

"*Therefore, as God's chosen people, holy and dearly loved, clothe yourselves with compassion, kindness, humility, gentleness, and patience.*"

I get it!

Boone ran after her, hoping to stop her before she went too far. The fog made it hard to see, but he kept going. He had to find her before something else happened.

"Kelly, where are you?"

He looked around frantically. Boone knew the danger that lurked; she did not. She seemed so innocent, naive. *Lord, help me find her then.*

She has to be here somewhere.

Then, out of the shadows, he saw it. A big male grizzly was wagging his head back and forth a few feet from Kelly. It paw-slapped the ground and huffed, blowing from its mouth.

"Kells...don't move!"

She froze in place and looked back at him.

The bear seemed agitated, but maybe it wouldn't charge if they could convince it they weren't a threat.

"Don't look him in the eyes. Back up slowly. If he charges, curl up and play dead. Whatever you do, DON'T RUN!"

Kelly slowly backed up until she got to Boone. He grabbed her hand and said, "Pray with me!"

"What?"

"Pray with me."

"*Yea, though I walk through the valley of the shadow of death, I will fear no evil: for thou art with me; thy rod and thy staff they comfort me.*"

"Make him go, Jesus!" Kelly added.

Within minutes, the bear retreated and ran off into the bush. Boone pulled Kelly to him and hugged her tightly. If anything happened to her, he'd never forgive himself. "Let's get out of this place!"

"Fine by me!"

THE PLAN

So, this is what we're going to do. We're going to follow the shoreline west. Hopefully, we'll find a cabin so we can call for help."

Parker looked annoyed. He was happy to have his feet untied, but still upset that his hands were tied. "Dude! I need my hands untied too!"

"Not on your life!"

"Maybe we should," Kelly told him. "What if another bear comes?"

Boone didn't want to think about it. He certainly didn't want to chance another encounter with Parker. Besides, Kelly didn't know what she was asking. The guy was a threat to her.

But then, something gnawed at him. Was he supposed to give the guy a second chance? After all, so many people gave him a second chance.

Boone decided to have a little chat with Parker first before deciding if he was going to untie his hands. He pulled him aside and whispered. "I'll untie you if you answer some questions."

"I can do that."

"What was going on in your head when you were choking Kelly?

If Parker didn't answer him with all honesty, he wouldn't untie the man. Boone could tell when someone was lying.

"Look, I get like this sometimes, man. I don't know what comes over me. I-I think I got the devil in me sometimes."

First answer, acceptable. Boone knew the carnal man. He was one before the Holy Spirit got hold of him. Sin still plagued him like everyone else. The only difference was that Jesus saved his sorry butt. Grace, it's what this guy needed, too.

"Next question." He kept his voice down so Kelly couldn't hear him. "And what were you planning to do to her? Were you gonna…?"

"Yes!" Parker cut him short. He nodded shamefully. "I-I'm sorry."

Boone wanted to kill him, but at least he admitted it. Sort of. It was the first time he heard the guy apologize.

"You will apologize to her before I untie you. Do you hear me? You will walk ahead of us at all times. And if I catch you even looking at her the wrong way, I will kill you."

Parker nodded.

Boone supervised the apology to Kelly. He watched the man show remorse. At least it looked genuine. Still, anyone can fake it, but he had to take the man at his word. That's where second chances start.

In his opinion, Kelly didn't take it very well. Not when he apologized for his intentions to assault her. She slapped his face when he said the dirty word. Boone was proud of her. She pushed past her timidity. He could tell she'd been through something like this before. That pained him to think of it.

Kelly needed a minute. She walked away from them both and sat on a rock. He'd leave her alone with her thoughts. Her prayers, too. She needed some time to process what happened.

Boone ordered Parker to gather supplies and tie them into the blankets. They'd need it at the next camp they made. He helped the man get the important things. *Lord, give me strength with this guy. Working together with him isn't going to be easy.*

While you're at it, help Kelly process the pain.

Once they were ready to go, Boone grabbed the orange flare gun and stuffed it into his hip wader pocket. That he was keeping with him. As soon as they got closer to civilization, he'd set it off. It only had a single flare, and he wanted to make sure someone saw it.

He also planned to use it if another bear got in his face. Or, if Parker pulls another stunt.

"Okay, people, let's move."

Parker took the lead, swinging the blanket of supplies over his shoulder. Boone swung supplies over his shoulder as well and walked side by side with Kelly. "Stay close!"

Kelly nodded.

If they were lucky, they'd stumble upon a trapper's cabin before nightfall. Boone knew it had nothing to do with luck, though. He could tell God was with them. *Direct our path, oh Lord!*

They would have to watch the tide. It would be high around 3 pm and low by 8 pm. He gathered it would make the lake edge difficult to maneuver, depending on the area they were walking through.

The last thing he wanted to do was bring them through the trees where the bears were more likely to be hanging out.

They trekked over boulders big and small as the lake water lapped the sandy edge. This was not going to be easy. They had to watch their footing. They had to keep going before they reached high tide.

"Can we stop?" Kelly moaned after a few hours. "My legs are killing me, and you guys walk too fast."

"Yah, let's take a break," Boone said, calling to Parker, who was way ahead. "Let's rest for a bit!"

So far, Parker was doing what he was told. He had led the pack since they left, without argument. Maybe there was hope for him yet.

Boone wiped sweat from his brow. The three of them sat on the rocky edge of the lake while birds greeted them with their voices. It was a beautiful place even under these circumstances.

"You know," Kelly smiled into the sun, "God sure made it pretty here."

Boone wanted to say, *He sure made YOU pretty,* but he held back because Parker was there.

"There is no God!" Parker said.

"Are you serious?" Kelly answered, annoyed. "You honestly believe there's no God? Who do you think made all this beautiful scenery?"

Boone was intrigued. It was an interesting twist to this whole nightmare. *God, are you telling me something here*? He himself claimed he was an atheist before he became a Christian. He'd jump in if need be, but right now, he wanted to see how Kelly handled this.

"Ever hear about the Big Bang Theory, honey? It's all about science."

"I know that's not true! I feel the presence of God in my life."

"Trust me, it's just your own head talking."

"No, it's not!" Kelly argued. "Boone? Tell him!"

Boone knew there was nothing he could say to convince the guy he was wrong. The only way to deal with an atheist was to demonstrate your own faith. That's exactly what he was going to do.

Time to jump in.

"Let me tell you a story," Boone grinned. "Once upon a time, I used to be like you. I had a dad I hated. He ruined my life. He ruined my mom's life. He was an alcoholic. I even blamed him for my mom's death."

"As a kid, I just wanted Superman to come kick my dad's butt, but he never did. Nobody came to save me. I was all alone. I was on my own in the worst kind of pain."

Both Kelly and Parker sat there wide-eyed and listened. Boone wondered if he should go on. It was difficult to sort through his painful memories, but it was necessary.

"Then one day, someone told me there was a God, and I said, nah, how could there be? If there was, surely he'd do something about my deadbeat dad by now. Surely he wouldn't let a little kid go through such agony. I told myself I wasn't going to believe in anything then."

"Time passed by, and little Boone grew into big Boone. He made a lot of mistakes. Then one day, he made the biggest mistake of his life. He broke the law and went to jail."

'Oh, Boone! I'm so sorry!" Kelly spoke softly.

"I knew it," Parker said, "you're a convict. You got that vibe about you!"

"Well, thanks for that, man!" Boone furrowed his brow. The guy's judgment made him feel small. Especially coming from someone like him.

"Anyway, while in jail, I saw things a man should never see." Boone looked at Parker, "You know what I'm talking about."

Boone choked back tears and tried to go on.

"I decided to give God another chance after Pastor Tom prayed with me. He runs a prison ministry. He said if I cry out to Jesus, he will help me. At first, I thought he was full of it. Where was this Jesus before? Nobody had saved me so far. But, against my better judgment, I decided to try. For the first time, I spoke to God."

"And nothing happened, right?" Parker mocked.

"On the contrary. That day, because I talked to God, it opened up a door to the most unimaginable love I'd ever experienced. Like Kelly said, you feel His presence when you finally believe. And that's what I did. I just believed. It was simple. Then I found myself talking to Him all the time."

"And then what happened?" Parker sneered. "Did this big man in the sky break you out of prison or something?"

"No! He made me stay there and finish my sentence."

"See!" Parker scoffed, "I told you. The big man in the sky doesn't exist."

"Well...because He made me go through my sentence, I learnt many lessons. He showed me that He will never leave me nor forsake me. He protected me from some of the most brutal assaults I've ever seen. My life was inches away from many attacks, yet he stopped them short and protected me instead."

"He saved me all right, just in a different way. I just kept praying. And now, I can honestly say he has never let me down. He has always come through for me every single time. Both in prison and now. There is no doubt in my mind that God exists. I am living proof."

Thank you, my Saviour!

"I soon learned that God is a God of second chances. He gave me strength when I was weak. Hope to carry on. He's my everything! He's a father when I need him. Much better than my earthly one. He tells me I'm never alone as long as I'm with Him. I told my convict self, if that's who God is, I want THAT!"

"The only reason I called myself an atheist before was because I was mad at God. I'm not mad anymore."

Parker was quiet. Boone could tell he was processing what he said. Should he push anymore? His words were telling. God used His story many times before. Would it work this time? He didn't know.

In the end, it was up to God!

THE LIE

The craggy shores of Kootznahoo Inlet proved unpredictable. It took all Kelly could do to trudge through the muck and rock. In most places, it was impassable. Large boulders poked out of the water's edge. Grasses and brush scraped against her body, slapping and preventing her from following the men as quickly as she wanted. They always seemed to get so far ahead of her.

Thankfully, she had good sturdy hiking boots. Boone had his hip waders that were securely fastened to his belt so they wouldn't come off. No doubt, the waterproof pants kept him dry. Parker was not so lucky. He lost his expensive loafers in the water when they crashed. Luckily, the rubber boots Boone borrowed from Ranger Jack were stuffed in one of the totes she found. Had it not been for them, he would still be in sock feet and not able to walk through the soggy terrain.

The journey reminded her of when she was a kid. She and her cousin would go wandering on hot summer days. There was this one place they nicknamed Rice Ball Lake. It was an alkaline lake, not at all like this one, but they walked the mucky water's edge through the reeds and cattails. The outcrops of marsh, lagoons, and bogs bordering this lake seemed so different from others. It was as if it weren't a lake at all, but a series of individual streams coming together.

Under different circumstances, this trek would be an adventure. But not now. Why hadn't anyone found them yet? Were they even searching for them? Maybe the plane sank. Boone told her both pontoons were damaged. Likely, that meant the plane couldn't stay afloat.

But didn't the plane have GPS? That's what she didn't

understand.

Kelly thought to ask Boone why the rescue was taking so long, but she didn't want to say anything. They'd been walking all day, and it was soon time to stop for the night. She liked the quietness. They had been talking on and off all day about all sorts of things. Boone seemed to be coaching Parker on Christianity. She hoped his interest was genuine. The guy was a chameleon. Yet, she was seeing a different side of him, *kind of.* It was odd, but maybe narcissists can change after all.

It was strange that they hadn't seen any signs of civilization, but Boone insisted they were very close to Angoon. If that was the case, why wouldn't there be cabins, or at least some sign of life, other than wildlife?

She had never been to Southeastern Alaska before, but Boone was from there, so he should know. From what he said, it was rough terrain. Unforgiving land, he told them. It was a place you could get lost in, and nobody would ever find you. That wasn't very reassuring. Yet, it was the truth. If he weren't with them, they would have no idea how to get out of these bogs.

They were at a junction that didn't even resemble a lake. It seemed like a large part of the lake had been reduced to a series of lagoons and streams with winding pathways. It was odd. She had no idea how boats would pass through these places. Maybe they didn't.

Maybe they were unreachable.

"Let's make camp in that inlet over there," Boone pointed to a weird flat spot to the right.

"Okay," she nodded out of breath. The sun was setting anyway. It looked like a safe enough place to spend the night, nestled against the water. She trusted Boone, and if he said it was safe from grizzlies, it was safe from grizzlies.

Kelly helped the guys get the fire going, and before she knew it, they were all huddled around a roaring fire with blankets draped around their shoulders. What little they did have for food was supposed to be their supper. She was thankful to at least have something, especially since none of them had much of anything to eat all day.

They each had a can of sardines and a bottle of water for supper.

"So, I don't get it. Why haven't they found us yet?" Kelly asked.

Boone was rolling back his sardine can, ready to scoop it into his mouth. "They better not be looking in the Kootznoowoo Wilderness."

"Why would they look there? Couldn't they tell we were right over water when we went down? Like, wouldn't the GPS tell them that?"

Boone was silent.

At first, Kelly thought he didn't hear her, but then she asked again. He still didn't answer.

Parker looked up and didn't say a word. He ate sardines like a ravenous wolf. Kelly could tell something was up, but she couldn't quite put her finger on it.

"Boone? What's wrong?"

Boone shook his head and kept on eating.

Kelly had finished hers already, and the guys were almost done. They both grabbed their bottled water and chugged it down. Kelly was no fool. She could tell something was wrong. Her intuition always told her so. If she had to guess, she'd say they had a secret.

"Okay, spit it out!"

Both men eyed each other.

"Tell her!" Parker said.

"Tell me what?"

Kelly looked back and forth from Boone to Parker, hoping someone would say something. Nobody did.

"C'mon!"

Then, Boone sighed. He set his empty sardine can down and looked straight at her. Then he hung his head and sighed again. This was serious. Kelly couldn't take it anymore. "Well, what is it? Spit it out!"

"They don't know where we are?"

"What? What do you mean they don't know where we are? How do you know that?

"Because my navigation system was destroyed by lightning before we even neared the water. We were still above wilderness territory when the lightning struck." Boone looked ashamed. "I'm sorry."

Kelly was dumbfounded. She didn't understand what he was implying. "I-I don't get it."

"What he's trying to tell you is nobody is coming to rescue us," Parker said matter-of-factly.

Tears started welling in her eyes. She made her aching body stand. Her legs felt like dead weights, and her feet were painful and bloody. How could this happen? Why did he make her believe they were going to find them if that wasn't the case?

"You mean, this whole time, you led me to believe they were coming, and now they're not? They have no idea where we are? I can't believe you, Boone. Why weren't you just honest with me? Why did you think you had to hide it from me? You obviously told Parker."

Parker had a smirk on his face. "You're in the doghouse now, buddy!"

"It's not funny, Parker! That means we're out here alone! LOST!"

Boone stood up and defended himself. "We're not lost! I know exactly where we are!"

"Yah! Sure you do!"

Kelly was in tears and exhausted. They had just spent the entire day pushing through bogs and reeds. She had wet, aching feet. When she checked, there was nothing but blood covering her socks. How was she supposed to push on tomorrow? That's what they were facing if nobody knew where they were. They would have to spend another day hiking. There was no way she could do this all again.

She had nothing left. She could not believe this!

Boone looked at Parker and shook his head.

"Don't look at me, buddy. You're on your own with this one!"

Kelly was not amused. This was serious. "Can a person even walk to Angoon? How many more days? What if I can't? You guys are stronger than I am."

"I'll carry you if I have to. You're a featherweight." Boone smirked."

"That's not funny," she said as she sniffed and wiped her tears. "Wouldn't they search a certain radius? Surely they would check all possible scenarios. I'm sure they're looking for us right now!"

"I didn't say they weren't looking for us," Boone said. "It might just take longer because they don't exactly know where we crashed."

"So, then they *are* coming! How long do you think it will take them?"

Boone scratched his beard and sighed, "It could take several days."

"Several days? NO! We don't have that long," Kelly cried in a panic. "Surely it will be sooner than that!"

"Kells... *Calm down.* This isn't helping!"

Kelly did not care. She couldn't be around these guys any longer. Even though it was almost dark, she needed some space to process this. She flung her arms in the air and stormed off toward the bushes without looking back.

"Where are you going?" Boone shouted after her.

"To the can!"

"Don't go too far. Remember what happened last time."

Boone said it was safe. There was nothing to worry about anymore. No bears here. She was taking him at his word. Though she didn't know how much his word meant now. *He lied!* Why didn't he just tell her the truth instead of getting her hopes up? *They were lost, and nobody was coming!*

All she could hear were two Neanderthals complaining about her as she walked off. Their voices echoed in the crisp night air. She had had enough of them already. She just wanted to go home! Kelly knew she was tired and overreacting, but she didn't care. She was completely and utterly exhausted.

Then, she heard Parker's insensitive words. "Women! Can't live with 'em, can't live without 'em!"

"I CAN HEAR YOU; YOU KNOW!" Kelly retorted. Maybe she could sleep somewhere else tonight!

Likely not

THE BABY

It was the wee hours of the morning when Kelly heard the cry. It sounded like a baby, but it couldn't be, not out here.

Last night, she got over her mad pretty quickly. All it took was a bit of rustling in the bushes to get her to make a beeline back to the two men who sat around the roaring fire.

The night air was cold and misty. Fog crept in again. They kept the fire roaring most of the night. Her place was between the two of them, even though she didn't like the idea at first.

Boone and Parker had gathered dry reeds to make a soft bed, so they had at least some protection from the dampness of the ground. They took a couple of wool blankets and laid them on top of the reeds. Then the other two blankets were draped over the three of them.

She didn't want to be in the middle, but shivering in the cold by herself was not an option. The men needed her warmth as much as she needed theirs.

And now, they were still sleeping as she lay awake listening to the baby cry. What could it possibly be? It was probably an animal. If Kelly didn't have to go to the bathroom so badly, she'd go back to sleep and ignore it.

Yet, it was hard to ignore such an alarming sound.

Maybe she could sneak out from between them. Boone's arm was around her, and Parker's back was facing her. They were both snoring and fast asleep.

Kelly lifted Boone's arm, trying not to wake him, but it was too late. She had disturbed him already. "Sorry, go back to sleep. I just need to pee."

"Don't go far."

"I won't."

She headed around the corner to the bush they were all using as a bathroom and figured it was pretty safe. She squatted down and relieved herself.

Then she heard it again. A baby cried in the fog. Could there be someone out there? Maybe they were in trouble? It sounded like it was coming from the middle of the lake. Was there a boat?

If there were a boat, maybe it would rescue them.

"Hello? Kelly called softly so she didn't disturb the men.

Rather than bothering them, she decided to go further. She'd go down shore just a little bit to see if she could see if there was a boat.

"Is there anyone out there?"

The fog made it hard to see, but she could still hear the baby crying. Was she going crazy? Maybe she was dreaming or sleepwalking.

Lord, what should I do?

Shivers went up her spine, and she froze in her tracks when she heard it even louder. She was getting closer to it.

Her gut told her to stop, *go back!* But she couldn't ignore the sound of a crying baby. Something was out there, and she had to find out what.

The mist sprinkled across her face as she squinted into the night. There was an outcrop of rocks ahead that overlooked the lake. It would make a good vantage point. Maybe she'd be able to see if there was a boat. Maybe a canoe. Could a boat have drifted away from a dock somewhere?

"Hello? Kelly called out as she climbed up. The lake was calm and pristine in the early morning. The sun was just peeking over the horizon, and she hoped the new light would help her see.

"Is there anyone out there?"

No answer.

The baby stopped crying. Maybe she was imagining it after all.

Kelly stood there on the rocks for a few minutes, peering into the water just to be sure, then she shook her head and climbed down. *Crazy!* She didn't realize she had wandered so far from camp.

What direction was it anyway? She wasn't sure.

Stepping into the wet sand with her hiking boots, she paused for a moment. The sun was coming from that way. That meant the camp was this way. Though, wasn't it by those bushes? She was all turned around. Tall, dark spruce lined the lake around her. It all looked the same.

In a panic, she hurried one way, then changed her mind and went the other way. Her heart beat wildly in her chest as she stopped to catch her breath.

What was that?

She heard something slap out of the water. She turned to see movement in the tall grass that followed a path to the tree line. It couldn't be a bear. It was something else.

Could it be a mother and baby? Maybe they were lost or disoriented. It's easy to do. Yet, it could be an animal, but she didn't think so. The swath through the reeds and cattails seemed large.

Then, she heard it again, a distinct baby cry. Now it was in the trees.

GO BACK!

Her gut told her one thing, but her head told her another. Maybe a mother and child were in trouble and didn't see her standing on the rock. She had to follow. It was the right thing to do.

"Hello?" she called. Kelly was in the tree line now. She stood in silence for a moment to listen. Was anyone out there? Or was this whole thing just her imagination playing tricks on her?

Again, a baby cried in the distance. This time, she also heard a whistle. It was very odd. It sounded like a low-high-low tone. Three distinctive whistles for sure.

That confirmed it. Someone was blowing a distress whistle. She followed it to investigate. She could now see a clear trail. And there was blood. *Oh Lord!*

What could have happened?

GO BACK!

Running through the forest, Kelly realized she was deep inside the tree line. She'd have to be careful of bears. She'd be quick. The sound was coming from just over that ridge. She was almost there.

The three-part whistle sounded again. Then, the baby cried.

As Kelly neared the corner, suddenly branches slapped her in the face. *What was that?* It stunned her and burned her cheeks, making her stumble backward. She couldn't see much of anything now.

Without warning, something hit her in the back of the head. She collapsed to the mossy forest floor with a thump.

A large figure reached down.

It was dragging her by the foot.

GIVE ME

The thing dragged her as it ran, body thumping through the forest. She fought, kicking and screaming at first, then unwittingly succumbed to its torture. Her limbs took the brunt of it, smacking through the forest underbrush, arms and legs limp in surrender.

Help me, Jesus!

It stopped for a moment and grunted. Then it continued down a slope, pulling Kelly like a rag doll. Her battered body lay numb, vulnerable. She couldn't see more than shadows of whatever had taken her.

It let out a loud, eerie shriek that echoed in what appeared to be a cave. It was damp and smelled foul, like something dead.

They rested there. Kelly breathed through throbbing pain. She could taste the iron in her own blood as it trickled into her mouth. The creature tied something around her eyes, then her wrists. *It was intelligent.*

She didn't dare speak.

All she could do was listen, wait, and push through the fear. Kelly figured if she could just remember to breathe, she'd be okay. She exhaled through pursed lips. *Breathe!* Then, she inhaled the pungent smell.

It was all she could do not to gag!

Kelly curled up into a ball as she scooted backward with her bum. The thing backed off, then came close again, sniffing. She could feel whiskers against her raw skin. Long, prickly hair dangled from its arms, brushing against her body. *Did it have fur?*

She shivered as it inhaled her aroma, panting like a dog. Kelly wreathed from its rank breath. She whispered a prayer,

"Jesus! Help me, please!"

It shrieked.

Oooh, it doesn't like that, she realized. She tried it again. This time, she recited the passage Boone used with the bear. It was the same one her Nana had taught her to recite as a kid, and she flippantly dismissed it.

"Yea, though I walk through the valley of the shadow of death, I will fear no evil: for thou art with me; thy rod and thy staff they comfort me."

"STOP!" it whimpered and retreated.

It can speak!

Kelly shivered, not wanting to provoke it further.

It came at her again, this time with force. It hurt her as it slammed against her body, forcing her down on the stale dirt floor. "GIVE!"

What did it mean?

"GIVE ME!"

The creature climbed on top of Kelly as she lay there paralyzed. Should she fight? Should she submit? What was it trying to do?

The creature had its foul-tasting mouth over her pursed lips. The fur was rough and scratchy. It was hurting her. All she could do was whimper against the pain as tears escaped her eyes under the blindfold.

It pulled away in frustration. "GIVE ME, NOW!"

She didn't know what it wanted. She froze, shaking uncontrollably.

"W-what do you want?!" she dared to ask.

The creature shouted, "YOU NO SPEAK!" It threw something big past her head. The object crashed to the ground beside her.

Again, it climbed on top of her. "GIVE SOUL!"

Her soul?

She could taste its foul breath. It was sucking. It pursed its mouth *hard* over her mouth and tried to suck her *soul!* It wanted her *soul!*

Jesus! ME!

The thing retreated immediately.

Kelly could breathe again. She licked her bloodied lips, then spit out the creature's slobber. She couldn't get the beastly taste out of her mouth. He was not charging at her again if she could help it! *"In the name of Jesus, leave me alone!"*

"Fear not, for I am with you," she quoted the memorized Bible verse. *"Be not dismayed, for I am your God. I will strengthen you, I will help you, I will uphold you with my righteous right hand!"*

The creature stayed at bay.

Thank you, sweet Nana, for teaching me to memorize.

Thank you, Jesus!

Kelly decided to pray continuously. It was her only defence at this point. If this thing didn't like it, that's what she'd do. She prayed she would be safe. She prayed the thing would go away. She prayed the guys would find her and rescue her. She prayed in Jesus' name.

The creature was still in the cave, but it was unusually quiet. She didn't know what it was doing. Was it thinking of its next move?

Kelly had to think fast. Could she sneak past? Which way was the way out? All she knew was she wasn't going anywhere with her hands tied and eyes covered.

She raised her tied wrists to her mouth and tried to chew through the rope. It was too thick. It would take hours at this rate.

It didn't matter. The thing was up again and in her face.

"Go away!" she told it.

"YOU NO SPEAK!"

"I am a child of the King! I am covered by the blood of Christ!"

It whimpered and withdrew.

It seemed like the moment she stopped praying or reciting Bible verses, the thing came forward again. Its obvious weakness gave her a huge advantage, one she needed if she was going to get out of there alive.

After Kelly tried to chew through the rope again, she

realized she had stopped praying. The creature immediately started growling. It circled her like she was prey. She knew she was in trouble. It was trying to outsmart her and find a way around her strategy.

"YOU NO SMART!" it said.

"No, but *God* is! Now leave me alone...*in Jesus' name!*"

The thing hissed and retreated, then slowly advanced again. This time, it grabbed Kelly by the hair and laughed. It pulled her to her feet and brought her face-to-face with it. "GIVE, OR DIE!"

"NO! Kelly cried, "I WILL NOT!"

The thing punched the side of her jaw. The blow dazed her, but she shook it off. She would not let it win. "You can NOT touch me! I belong to Jesus Christ!"

The thing shrieked again, then let go of her hair. It threw her down to the ground like a discarded dishrag. Would he finally leave her alone? Or, would they play this game all day?

It seemed hopeless.

Kelly sobbed as she lay there crumpled on the ground. She realized, short of a miracle, the creature was going to find a way to kill her.

Lord Jesus, I need a miracle.

"STOP!"

Could it even hear her thoughts?

Then, suddenly, Kelly heard something else approach. It sounded like a bear in the cave with them. A BEAR? There was no escaping this. Her life was about to end.

"Jesus, help!"

The bear growled, and the creature hissed. Kelly heard them both charge each other, fighting only a few feet away from her. The vicious attack thundered through the cave. One animal attacked the other, the pair huffing and snorting.

Now! I gotta go now!

Kelly inched against the wall, trying to find a way around the angry beasts. Without knowing which way to escape, it was virtually impossible.

Then a squeal. Then a whimper. Then silence.

Everything went still. Who was dead? Was it the bear or the creature? Kelly didn't know. She froze. Should she make a run for it and hope they were both dead? *Not likely.* One of them was still alive. It didn't really matter which one. She was dead either way.

Terrified, Kelly stood there listening. All she could hear was the thumping sound of her own heartbeat in her ears. What was happening? *Am I next?*

Then, she heard it clear as day. One of them was eating the other. *My God, this is shocking!* She could hear flesh ripping apart. The ravenous beast chomped and chewed loudly, as if it had a point to prove to her.

Was it the bear? Or was it the creature?

Kelly hyperventilated a she listened to the feasting. *Breathe!* She stayed as still as possible. Maybe the victor wouldn't notice if she slipped away. *Maybe.*

She inched along the wall slowly, *slowly!*

When she came upon something hard, she accidentally knocked it over. *BANG!* The feasting suddenly stopped. *Oh, NO!*

Whoever the victor was had just noticed her. Was it the bear or the beast? She had no clue.

"YOU STAY!" the eerie voice commanded.

Kelly gasped. The brutal truth revealed itself, *Bears don't talk.*

It was the thing!

JUST BELIEVE

Boone awoke in a panic when he realized Kelly was missing. Where was she? He must have drifted back to sleep after she left to go to the bathroom.

That was a while ago.

He knocked Parker awake, hoping he knew where she was. "Hey, Parker! he said, pushing at his back, "Where's Kelly?"

"I don't know, dude! Let me sleep!"

Boone's mind raced. He looked around the camp, but the fog had settled in overnight. Visibility was near zero. A cool mist was falling, and it was overcast.

"GET UP!" Boone shouted this time.

Parker bolted upright, blurry-eyed, shivering in the blanket. Boone needed his help. They had to find her. She could be anywhere in this fog. With bears everywhere, she was in imminent danger.

He'd take the flare gun!

"KELLY!" he shouted, "WHERE ARE YOU?!"

By then, Parker was putting his rubber boots on. Boone already had his hip-waders pulled up and was fastening them to his belt, tucking the flare gun into his pocket. He threw his ball cap on and was ready to go.

Lord, help us find her, he prayed.

Thunder cracked in the distance. They were in for another storm. It was an on-and-off again thing in these parts. They'd have to hurry or they'd never be able to follow her tracks.

Something in the pit of his stomach told him she was in danger. It didn't feel right. Last night, when she went to the bathroom, he remembered her calling to them. Or was that just a dream?

Stupid, Boone! How could you fall back asleep? How could you let her wander off again?

"Leave the stuff!" Boone ordered Parker, who was rummaging around trying to find something. "We'll come back for it later."

"How do you know she isn't just pissing in a bush somewhere?"

Boone wanted to hit the guy. "Because I KNOW!"

"Okay, okay," Parker said, "you don't have to bite my head off. I'm just asking. "Sheesh!"

Boone and Parker headed off into the fog as they followed her tracks. The mist made it slippery, but he could still see her footprints.

"Don't tell me, you know how to track, too?" Parker guffawed as he followed Boone.

"Of course I do!"

"Man, is there anything you *can't* do?"

Boone wanted to say, *Yeah, shut you up!* But he didn't. *Lord, give me strength.* This guy irritated him quite easily. He needed to keep a clear head. Finding Kelly was his top priority.

They followed her tracks to the toilet bush, then off downriver to an outcrop of rocks that overlooked the lake.

"Looks like she climbed up here?" Boone pointed to muddy scuff marks leading to the top of the rocks. "What was she doing?"

He climbed up to see the vantage point. It overlooked the widest part of the lake. Boone hoped he didn't see a body floating below the rocks. He prayed under his breath that it wasn't so. Thankfully, nothing like that was in the water.

The foggy lake echoed their voices as they called out her name. Both of them left the rock formation and kept on. So far, no Kelly. No answers at all.

"Look!" Boone pointed, "Something came out of the water here and dragged itself to shore."

"Did she go swimming or something?" Parker asked earnestly. This time he was serious. Boone could tell he was genuinely concerned, like he was.

"I don't know, but let's find out. The trail looks like it leads to the tree line."

What were you doing, Kells-Bells?

Boone noticed two sets of tracks. One was Kelly's hiking boots, the other was a paw print of some kind.

He feared the worst now. This was not good!

"KELLY!" they both yelled, "WHERE ARE YOU?"

Boone kept seeing hair along the trail, but it wasn't Kelly's. It wasn't blonde, it was dark brown and grey. It wasn't human, that's for sure. He deliberately didn't say anything to Parker until he knew.

This was something else.

They reached the tree line and went deep into the spruce and hemlock. Both sets of tracks ended about five hundred feet inside the forest. He could see a trail. Then, Boone saw the obvious struggle. *Blood!*

Something had taken her.

"Okay, you see that?" Boone pointed as he knelt in the flora. He sighed, realizing he had to tell Parker what he was thinking.

Parker knelt and touched the blood. Kelly's hair was caught between the twigs. The area looked like it was a battleground. She must have fought pretty hard. *Oh Lord, please help her!* Bloody blonde hair was all over, but so was the brown and grey hair.

Thunder cracked directly above them. The mist had turned to a soft rain. The trail would be washed out soon. They had to hurry. But first, Boone needed to tell Parker something. He brought him over to a wide-branched spruce and took shelter under it.

"Look, there's a legend around here," Boone hesitated, "They call it the Kushtaka, or Kooshdaa kaa, in Tlingit. It means land-otter-man. I seriously think that's what took her."

Boone watched Parker's eyes grow big, then he burst out laughing. "You mean to tell me a Sasquatch got her?" He roared so loudly that the ravens flew away.

"Keep your voice down!"

"Dude, you're losing it. First, it's this Jesus stuff, now it's the boogeyman. What's next?"

Boone was disappointed. He thought he was making headway with the guy yesterday. He seemed interested in Christianity, but apparently not.

That wasn't his problem.

Right now, he just had to convince him that a mythical creature from Tlingit folklore had abducted Kelly. *Oh boy!* Boone didn't even know if he believed it himself.

He never even saw one before, but he heard plenty of stories. Many who go missing in Southeastern Alaska are said to be taken by the Kushtaka.

The creature is supposed to be part otter, part man. They say it's a shapeshifter and can become anything, even mimic a baby crying. It lures people lost in the wilderness, pretending to be a helpless child or woman in distress. Then, it takes their soul.

Can't have mine! It's already taken! Boone told himself.

Boone didn't know how much of that was true anyway. All he knew was that the Bible speaks of Nephilim. They were offspring of fallen angels and human women. Giants. In this case, a giant otter-man.

Boone wrestled with the thought. Whatever it was, it had Kelly. He and Parker were tracking it. It looked like the creature dragged her to its den.

"Stop!" Boone whispered, pointing out a dip in the valley. "The trail leads over there. We need to hold back and wait. Let's see what we're dealing with before we go any further."

"It's probably just a bear," Parker said.

"No, it's not! You think a bear has hair like this?" Boone held up long strands of animal hair, unlike anything he'd ever seen before.

Boone decided they'd climb an old Sitka spruce to get a better vantage point. He was glad he brought the rope. He quietly flung it high into the tree branches.

"You go first," he told Parker. Boone explained how to do it.

This way, they had a better vantage point and a safe place to hide. If Kelly were there, they'd know pretty soon.

Once Parker got himself up and found a secure branch to rest upon, Boone heaved himself up as well. He drew the rope to him, hiding it so it wasn't visible anymore. Now they wait.

If she's alive, God, please let us find her soon.

Thunder cracked above. The spruce protected them from the rain and served as a hideout, but the tradeoff was not fun. The spruce needles were sharp, and the sticky sap was messy.

They were up there for an hour before the fog lifted. The rain had stopped, and Boone could see clearly from that position.

Then, out of the shadows, a figure appeared. Boone shushed Parker. "Look!" he pointed, "over there on the ridge. Do you see it?"

"It's a bear!" Parker said.

"No, it's not! Now, *shush!*"

The two of them sat perched in the spruce tree. The creature inched forward like it knew they were there. Its mouth was covered in blood. It stopped just before the tree and sniffed into the air. Then, it stood on its hind legs and growled.

"Jesus! Protect us!"

The enormity of the creature was unsettling. It was the biggest otter he'd ever seen. It had the face of a man, yet the body of an otter. It suddenly let out a piercing cry, mimicking a baby.

Parker looked wide-eyed at Boone. He didn't have to say anything. He could read the man's face like a book. He sure believed him now.

The Kushtaka was real!

THE BIRDS

L et's get down and follow it," Boone told Parker.

"No way, I think I'll stay right here."

That thought had crossed Boone's mind too after seeing the ugly creature, but if Kelly was in its lair, they had to help her.

The Kushtaka disappeared back into the bushes, but its trail was still fresh. Boone knew he could track it. "Let's go!"

Boone used the rope and rappelled down the tree. He held it in place so Parker could follow. Reluctantly, the man lagged behind him, even though, for a moment, he thought he was going to abandon him.

"It went this way," Boone pointed out.

The two men headed in that direction until they came upon a clearing. Then, suddenly, a flock of ravens landed around them. It was odd, like they were surrounding them deliberately for some reason.

"What the heck?"

Boone backed up against Parker, and the two stood in place as the ravens circled them. They danced on the forest floor, coming closer and closer, taunting them with their croaking and cawing.

Then, suddenly, they all took flight at once and spiraled around them. Round and round they flew, pecking at them. It was a deliberate attack.

Boone tried to protect his face and head by raising his arms, but they bit them instead. Parker did the same, but it was hopeless. The ravenous mob of birds would not let up.

"Run!" Boone cried.

The two of them ran through the forest, and the birds

followed them in attack mode. They pecked at them until they fell to the ground.

"*Jesus! Make them stop!*" Boone cried.

Suddenly, they were gone. There was no explanation for it. Boone thought maybe this, too, was the Kushtaka. They were known to shape-shift and take on different forms. Did it know they were hiding in the trees?

Boone figured maybe it did.

Then, as the men sat there to collect themselves, a large figure bolted from the bushes. "Go! Go! Go!" Boone yelled at Parker to get out of there fast.

They limped and staggered in the opposite direction as the creature pursued them, but it was too late. They had no chance. It was there in seconds with another beside it.

Kushtaka! Two of them!

Boone booted one of them in the head, but it didn't do any good. The other one slugged him hard until he dropped to the ground. It dragged his body through the rough underbrush.

Parker was attacked as well. He went limp beside him as he was dragged by the smaller one. He looked like he was unconscious.

Jesus! Help!

Both beasts stopped for a moment and shrieked at each other. He pretended to play dead as his bruised body bounced around on the cold, wet ground.

Inside his hip wader pocket, the flare gun was hiding, and his pocket knife was clipped to his belt. He'd use them as soon as he had the opportunity.

They stopped just before the two creatures entered what looked like a cave. Boone peeked out of one eye, then closed it. If they thought he was out cold, maybe he could gain an advantage somehow.

As they dragged him and Parker into the cave, Boone opened one eye again. There she was. *Kelly!* She was badly beaten, but Boone could tell she was still alive.

She flinched when they pulled his body near her.

She had a blindfold on and her hands were tied. He quickly assessed the situation before they noticed he was conscious.

There, in the corner, a large dead bear lay half ripped open. He could see its exposed ribcage and entrails. It looked like they had been feasting on the carcass for quite of while.

Boone realized the extent of their strength. To take down a grizzly of that size, they would have to be extremely powerful. But then, there were two of them against one bear.

Looking up, Boone could see a hole, exposing sunlight. That told him they were deep under the forest floor. They were in a cave or cavern of some sort.

Water trickled down the side wall and seemed to escape somewhere. They must be near an underground spring. That meant fresh water. That was good. He made a mental note of that.

As he lay there playing dead, he saw one of the creatures come at him with a rope. It tied his hands. He peeked one more time and saw Parker start to move. *Good, he's alive!* Then Boone was blindfolded like Kelly and propped up next to her.

He reached over and held her hand, squeezing it softly. "It's gonna be okay," he whispered, trying not to alert the creatures who now sounded like they were feasting on the bear again.

Kelly let out a whimper and responded with a squeeze. "Is Parker here too?"

"Yes!"

"There's something you need to know," she whispered, "they're afraid of Jesus. Call His name and they won't touch you."

Boone squeezed her hand.

What were they dealing with here? *Afraid of Jesus?* Were they demons? Of course they were, especially if they were Nephilim. That would explain a lot about the Kushtaka legend.

Call His name, and they won't touch you. What had they tried to do to Kelly? What were they intending to do with him and Parker? They had to get out of there, but he had to be smart about it. They were strong.

Suddenly, a voice shouted, "GIVE ME!"

"They can talk?"

Kelly squeezed his hand. "Shhh!"

The beast seemed to be harassing Parker. "Get off of me, you pig!" he said, following that with a list of swear words.

All Boone could hear was a bunch of screaming and moaning. Patrick was resisting them. It sounded like he was giving them all he had, but they were still winning. He could hear them slugging him repeatedly.

"GIVE ME, NOW!"

Then Kelly shouted, "Get off of him! *In Jesus' name!*"

Both beasts stopped suddenly. The small one with a female voice shrieked and cried all the way out of the cave. Only one remained.

Then, it was Boone's turn. It pulled him flat on his back. He decided not to fight, lying perfectly still in hopes it would leave him alone. But it didn't. Instead, the monster crawled on top of him and put its mouth on his mouth. *Oh, this was not happening!*

The Kushtaka tried to suck up his breath or something. Boone gagged and choked and spat back. He paid for that one. It smacked him hard across the face, leaving a taste of blood in his mouth.

"GIVE ME SOUL!"

"My soul? So, that's what you want," Boone scoffed and remembered what Kelly told him. "My soul belongs to Jesus Christ!" he shouted. "YOU CAN'T HAVE IT!"

The creature immediately squealed and got off of him.

Boone remembered his pocket knife clipped to his belt. Could he grab it with his hands tied? It was on his right side. If he could reach it he could get his hands free, then grab the gun stuffed in his pocket.

The Kushtaka came back and started sniffing him. He stopped what he was doing and froze. There was no way it was pulling that stunt again. He would not let it assault him!

"Go away, you freak!" he spat. "I belong to Jesus Christ, and you have no power over the living God!"

The Kushtaka retreated, but it went for Parker instead. He

could hear him screaming now. "PARKER!" Boone shouted, "Use the name of Jesus! He can't touch you if you say, Jesus!"

"DO IT!" Kelly shouted frantically.

Parker screamed. Boone envisioned the thing lying on the man, doing the same thing it did to him. "Say it, Parker! Say, Jesus!"

"GIVE SOUL!"

Boone heard it trying to suck out his soul.

Parker cried, *"Jesus Christ!"* in between gurgling sounds. But the creature wouldn't stop. It kept on assaulting him.

"Why isn't it working?" Kelly screamed, *"Jesus! Save him!* SAVE PARKER!"

It was then that Boone realized, *"We can't say it for him."*

Parker screamed and choked. It was hard to hear. Muffled sounds escaped the man's throat like he was drowning, as the monster stole his soul. *Lord, God Almighty!*

"MINE!" the Kushtaka roared victoriously.

Horrified, Boone knew...*Parker was gone.*

THE ESCAPE

Boone whittled away at the rope with his knife. He could move his hands more freely, but it wasn't off of him yet. Just a little bit longer.

Kelly was quiet. He could tell she was traumatized after hearing them torture Parker to death. Hearing was sometimes much worse than seeing, especially if you experienced the same kind of assault.

Boone knew she had. "You okay?"

Kelly didn't answer. She softly wept beside him.

Thankfully, the beasts were preoccupied with the bear carcass again. The female one came back after her mate had killed Parker. He could hear them cooing. Boone's stomach churned at the sound of it. These beings were intelligent, part human, part animal. But make no mistake, they were definitely evil.

"Don't worry, I'll get us out of here if it's the last thing I do!"

The weeping continued.

The rope was coming apart. Boone pushed the blade to the limit until it released his hands. He wriggled his wrists out of the prickly rope and lifted his blindfold immediately.

There they are!

Two Kushtaka lay down beside the bear carcass. They appeared to be sleeping. He could see their beastly chests rise and fall. If they were going to get out of here, they'd have to go now.

"Kells! It worked!" he whispered as he untied her hands. She rubbed her bloodied wrists and lifted her blindfold.

Boone looked her over. Streams of tears ran pathways down her cheeks through blood and dirt. Her lip was cut, and her face was bruised on both sides. Her blonde hair stuck to her bloodied scalp, but her distinguished beauty still enlightened him. He smiled and held her face in his coarse hands. "You're okay!"

Kelly's striking blue eyes thanked him, moving softly into a kiss. They held each other, bloodied foreheads pausing together, for just a moment. Boone realized for the first time just how much he loved this woman. *I need to get her out of here!*

The two of them stood, hand in hand, as they shimmied against the cave wall past the beasts. *Quiet!* They had to move with precision, or they'd wake them up.

"Shhh," Boone whispered, motioning to Kelly as they tiptoed to the clearing where they came in. From there, it was just a few more feet around the corner to the outside.

Suddenly, they were free.

They found themselves under the canopy of spruce trees once again. It was dusk, and they were losing light. They would have to move fast. Should he take her back to camp? Would they be safe there? Not likely if the Kushtaka had lured her from there.

Boone hadn't thought this far ahead.

Where do I go, Lord? He prayed under his breath.

They were both hurt pretty badly. Kelly was limping, and a couple of her fingers were broken. She looked like she had taken quite a beating, so he wanted to find a place for her to rest.

"Keep going, Boone," she told him.

"Don't you need to rest?"

Kelly shook her head, "Not with those things out there, I don't. Let's just keep going as far as we can. How far do you think Angoon is?"

"Twenty miles west, maybe."

"That's it? How long would that take us?"

Boone knew where she was going with this, but she was in no condition to travel twenty miles on foot. He'd end up having to carry her. That wouldn't be such a bad idea if it weren't for his pecked-up arms. The ravens sure did a number on his wrist.

"With your injuries? Too long!"

The two of them continued through the trees. He hoped they would make it to the water by the time it got dark. If the sun went down and they were still in the forest, they were vulnerable to bear attacks as well as those two ugly creatures.

Boone preferred not to meet up with either one.

"C'mon, Boone! I can do it. Let me try! If I can get through *that,* I can get through anything. Besides, what other choice do we have?"

Against his better judgment, Boone agreed. There was no safe place in the Alaskan wilderness. She was right. What other choice did they have? "Okay, let's go. But you do as I say, when I say it. Are we clear?"

"Yes, sir!" Kelly saluted. She was trying to tease him, but it wasn't funny. They were still in a lot of danger, and he didn't need her wandering off again. If anything happened to her, he'd never forgive himself.

As the sun set, they made it out of the tree line to the water's edge. The moon was out, and the weather was finally tolerable. No fog tonight, so it was clear enough to see miles ahead. That was a good thing.

They walked for hours, only stopping for a few minutes to rest along the way. He helped her walk when she needed it, and left her alone when she said she could do it herself. She was a fighter.

Boone thanked the Lord for her. She was a blessing to him. He watched her limp along in front of him as he trailed behind. She was a petite little thing. Nothing but skin and bones. He wondered how she even made it through such a nightmare.

Even under these harsh circumstances, beaten and torn up, she was beautiful. The moonlight showed him just how beautiful she was, with her hair glowing, her figure defined. God made her just for him. He knew it!

Thank you, Jesus!

They dragged their feet forward into the early morning. Twenty-four hours had passed since Kelly's abduction. Were the Kushtaka still following them?

Boone kept looking back. He thought he saw something a couple of hours ago, but not anymore. He figured it was safe to stop and rest a bit. Maybe longer this time.

"Let's rest here a bit."

"We can't! What if they're still following us?"

Boone tried to calm her nerves. They sat on an outcrop of boulders at the water's edge. All she needed was rest. He needed it too. Just half an hour. They were running on empty.

"Kells, it's okay! They're gone!"

She still looked worried, so he figured he'd change the mood and tell her about his aunt Sally's Tlingit delicacies. "So, I figure I should warn you. Once we get to Angoon, my aunt will offer you some stink eggs. Ever have them?"

"What eggs?"

"Stink eggs," Boone chuckled, "they're a Tlingit delicacy. They're fermented herring eggs. They're pretty smelly, and they taste terrible. Kind of like rotten chicken eggs, but they're fish eggs."

"You're making this up!"

"No, I'm serious!" he chuckled, "I don't recommend them at all."

"No doubt," Kelly laughed. "Who would eat something that gross?"

"Me."

Boone liked teasing her. He especially liked seeing her in a better mood than before. Laughing was good for the soul. Something he was glad they both still had. He thanked God for that one!

They talked about all kinds of things after that. Hopes. Dreams. Faith. Family. It was so easy to talk to her, like she understood him. She got his jokes, and that was a feat in itself. Nobody got his jokes.

The two of them talked longer than intended. They'd have to get going again. He was sure they were only a few miles from Angoon. This would be over soon.

A cheery robin suddenly chirped as dawn broke, telling

them it was time to go. The wind was picking up anyway, which told him rain was coming again. Hopefully, they'd be in Angoon by then.

Boone knew they needed medical attention as soon as possible. Though Angoon didn't have a hospital, the local doctor would have to suffice. His aunt was a trained nurse as well before she retired.

He planned to shoot the flare gun as soon as they were close enough to civilization. They were designed to be visible even in bright sunlight. Hopefully, someone would see it and come rescue them.

The State Troopers and the Coast Guard were probably still looking for them. Likely too far east. He knew the closest help was Angoon.

All they had to do was get there.

THE PLAN

Kelly's body ached all over, but she kept going. She wasn't going to tell Boone that. She didn't want him to stop and set up camp at all, not with those things still out there. All she wanted was to get to Angoon.

She was still trying to wrap her head around what happened to Parker. Sure, she didn't like him, and she had good reason to, but he didn't deserve to die like that.

It was horrific.

His painful cries still haunted her. She tried everything to shake it, but she just couldn't. Talking to Boone helped. He had a way of calming her down. She liked that.

Lord, help me forget!

The sun was out, yet it didn't feel that way. It was a heavy overcast, and she knew they were in for another rainy day. By the sounds of it, they were just a few miles out of Angoon.

They couldn't get there soon enough.

At this point, Kelly was moving like a turtle. Her feet were numb, wet, and cold. Her legs ached, especially her left one. She didn't know if her ankle was sprained or broken. One thing was for sure: she knew two fingers were badly broken. The pain was unbearable.

C'mon, Kelly, keep going! She told herself.

"Are you okay?" Boone asked, offering to help her.

"I'm fine!"

"You're not fine! You can barely stand. Let me carry you on my back for a while."

Kelly realized she had no choice. Her mind told her she could do it, but it wasn't listening to her body. She figured if she took one more step, she'd pass out.

"Okay," she teetered, nearly falling over, "but what about your arm?"

"What about it?"

"Has it stopped bleeding yet?"

She knew he was covering up the fact that he was leaving a trail of blood again. She was no nurse, but she was an aide, and she saw her share of wounds. The raven's attack had ripped open a vein in his wrist. Though he made a makeshift tourniquet to stop the bleeding, it wasn't holding anymore. "Boone, let me tighten it before you carry me, or we'll both pass out."

Boone was stubborn; she'd give him that. If he didn't let her help him, he could bleed to death. No way was that happening. She needed him as much as he needed her.

"Fine, but you're making a big deal out of nothing. Your injuries are much worse than mine."

"What, are we comparing battle wounds now?" she chuckled as she took his arm and tightened the tourniquet. "There, now tell me next time if it starts gushing again instead of being so stubborn."

"Yes, Mom!"

They both chuckled now.

As he heaved her up on his back to give her a piggy-back ride, she thought she heard something. Was it a bird? Maybe it was an eagle. She looked around from her taller vantage point on his back but couldn't see anything.

Maybe she was paranoid. She had good reason to be. She tried to ignore her anxiety as they went along for about half an hour like that.

Then she heard it again. A strange bird call.

Kelly looked into the tree line to see if she could see anything. Nothing. She looked toward the water and saw nothing. She looked as far as she could see in front of her, and only saw the sand, reeds, and grass lining the lake. Nothing was out of the ordinary.

"Man, you're heavier than you look," Boone joked.

"Maybe you're just too weak," she teased.

He started running to prove her wrong, but her body didn't like the piggyback now. Her head throbbed as it bobbed up and down. "Okay, okay, slow down! You proved your point."

He set her down and laughed, winded and tired. "Boy, that was easier when I was a whole lot younger."

"You're not old!"

Then she heard it again. The sound. This time it was evident. It wasn't a bird, it was a baby.

"THEY'RE HERE!

"What? Where?"

"I don't know, I just hear the baby."

Boone spun around so fast. He looked in all directions for anything out of the ordinary. She couldn't remember if she told him that's how it all started.

"It's not a baby!"

"I know!"

They both paused, listening for the sound.

Then, in the distance, out on the water, just like before, a baby cried. This time, she wasn't going to be so naive.

"It's in the water, Boone! They're coming for us!"

Kelly knew they had to run. She knew it was only a matter of time before the monsters would take them again. This time, they wouldn't be so lucky.

Jesus! Help us one more time!

They hurried along as fast as they could, but it wasn't fast enough. Kelly's leg wouldn't work right, and her ankle gave her excruciating pain. She fell behind Boone.

"Go! Just go without me!" she cried.

The two creatures slithered to shore about eight hundred feet north of them. She could see them heading straight for them.

"I will NOT leave you behind!" he grabbed her hand and pulled her along. They were slow, but they were going. Kelly figured the creatures would catch up to them in no time at all.

She pushed her aching body and ignored the pain. Her ankle wouldn't move like normal, but she forced it to behave. It had to.

Their only hope was to get away from them as fast as they could.

Then, in the distance, they saw something else in front of them. Three grizzlies stood on shore about a mile up the sandy beach. Maybe the bears wouldn't notice them. Maybe they could run past them unharmed?

"Look!" she cried.

"I see them!"

"What do we do?

"Pray!" Boone shouted.

Kelly prayed with everything she had. She prayed loud and bold. *"Jesus, remove them from our path! Get us to safety!"*

The longer they ran, the closer they got to the bears. The monsters were gaining on them as well. When they couldn't go any further, they stopped to catch their breath. They were caught between the beasts.

"What do we do now?

He looked around, trying to come up with a plan. He peered into the forest, then to the water. "I got it! I got a plan!"

She looked at him, puzzled, worried that the monsters were almost there. The bears were near them, too. Kelly and Boone were smack dab in the middle of it all.

"What's the plan? Hurry!"

"The enemy of my enemy is my friend, right? Let's let them battle it out with each other while we take a nosedive in the lake."

"Seriously! That's your plan? The water is ice cold, and we wouldn't last long in there either with the current. Plus, bears are good swimmers. So are those two things."

"You got a better idea? We have no choice!"

The two waited until just the right moment. They got as close to the bears as they dared and hid behind a big outcrop of rocks. Then they waited for the two monsters to come.

"They have to run into each other. *Wait!*"

Kelly knew this was their only option, but it was a dangerous one. She knew they had one shot at this. *"Jesus, let this work!"*

"See that log floating in the lake?" Boone pointed, "That's our destination. When I say go, we head for the lake. We'll meet up at the log if we get separated."

"Ready?" Boone asked as he viewed the situation coming to a head. "GO, GO, GO!"

Boone took her hand and pulled her into the cold water. They waded in as the bears looked at them. "SWIM, KELLY, SWIM!"

The water was deep now, and she couldn't touch the bottom. She swam with all her might as she watched the scene play out on the shore. The three grizzlies went into full-on attack mode with the two creatures. It was a violent and vicious attack.

Boone made it to the log ahead of Kelly. He hung on with one arm, waiting for her to reach him. But she couldn't. The current was too strong. It was sucking her down. "Boone! Help!"

She waved her arms at him and then went fully under, flailing and choking in the water. The current had a hold on her, and it wouldn't let go either.

Jesus, ME!

It was too late. He had abandoned her, just like everyone did in her life, she thought. He left her to fend for herself. Why? What was this all for?

Kelly took her last breath as she went under. Bubbles escaped her mouth for the last time as her head slipped beneath the surface of the water. This was it.

She was finally going home.

SOMEONE SEE

Boone couldn't find her. He dove deep, again and again, but she was nowhere in sight.

Jesus! Please!

He looked all over, but she hadn't surfaced anywhere. Where could she be? He took another breath and went under. He swam in all directions, but couldn't find her.

Was she gone?

Don't take her, Lord!

He tread water, shaking his head. His plan had failed. He had failed. She was so vulnerable, and he lost her. *He lost her!*

Boone cried in anger. "Why, God, WHY?"

He started swimming back to the log when he noticed something on the opposite side of the shore. It was her. IT WAS HER! The current swept her to the other side. Boone swam with all his might. Luckily, the lake was narrow enough and it wouldn't take long. PUSH! FASTER!

Boone was right there. HE WAS RIGHT THERE!

Was he too late? Had it been too long? He dragged her body flat and started performing CPR. He opened her airway. Checked for breathing. None. He remembered the *thirty-and-two-no-matter-who rule* from his training. He counted the chest compressions and gave two rescue breaths.

Nothing. "Come on, Kelly! *Breathe!*"

Again. Thirty chest compressions, then two breaths. "*Breathe!*"

Still nothing.

"*God! PLEASE!*"

Thirty chest compressions, then two breaths. Again, thirty chest compressions, then two more breaths. "Come on, Kelly!

Come back to me! BREATHE!"

He tried one more time, *"In the name of Jesus Christ, breathe!"* He compressed her chest thirty more times, then gave her two more puffs of breath. "Breathe, Kelly, breathe!"

Then, suddenly, she choked up water.

SHE WAS ALIVE!

"Thank you, Jesus! *Thank you, Jesus!"*

He rolled her over on her side as she vomited more water. Then he cradled her head in his hands and wept, the hardest he ever wept for anyone. "Don't you ever do that to me again!"

"I saw Jesus! He was beautiful! He had fire eyes!"

"Oh, Kelly! He kissed her on the lips. He brought you back to me. He brought you back to me!" he wept.

She sat up and looked stunned. "I'm okay? I thought you abandoned me. I-I thought..."

"Shhh," Boone told her, "You're okay! Just rest!" He sat beside her with his arm around her on the beach. He brought her head to rest on his shoulder and just sat there with her. *This is enough. This whole thing is enough.*

Across the water from them, down the beach a way, Boone saw the aftermath of blood and mayhem. The three bears had won. The Kushtaka were both dead, and the bears were feasting on them.

Good riddance!

They were still not out of danger yet, but Boone decided they couldn't go any further. Either they would be rescued or they wouldn't be. There was no way they were making it to Angoon on foot now.

He decided to shoot the flare gun right where they sat.

It was still securely tucked into the side pocket of his hip waders. Hard to believe he didn't lose it along the way, but he was thankful now for his special order pants with all the pockets. They were worth their weight in gold.

It was time.

Boone got the orange gun out, raised it to the overcast sky, and shot it. The bright flare illuminated the Alaskan wilderness below. *God, let someone see it. We have nothing left. We need a rescue!*

Kelly was in shock. She needed medical attention fast. She had very little strength. She couldn't even hold herself upright. She was losing body heat fast, and now it was beginning to rain.

For the first time, Boone realized they may die there. He felt defeated. They had been through so much for it to end this way. God got them through everything. He protected them from a plane crash, a bear attack, and a raven attack. He saved Kelly from drowning. He helped them defeat monsters for Pete's Sake. This couldn't be the end. *I just met her.*

God, let someone see the flare!

Boone thought about the spiritual implications of everything that happened. That alone was profound. So many lessons. So many near misses. *God, you were right there the whole time.*

When you call, He comes.

He can honestly say, God has never let him down. Not once!

I'm the one with shortcomings. You have never failed me, Jesus! Not even in my darkest depths did you abandon me. You're a perfect father! One I completely trust.

But by the grace of God go I.

Three people died. That could have been him. It could have been Kelly. Yet, it wasn't. Why wasn't it?

Even in the cave, saying the name of Jesus protected him and Kelly from the monsters, but not Parker. Why?

Because Parker's soul didn't belong to God.

He answered his own question. Boone's soul was bought and paid for by the blood of Jesus Christ. So was Kelly's. Evil couldn't take it!

He also knew the power of the blood. He knew just saying the name of Jesus was powerful, but only to those who believe. He and Kelly believed. Parker did not.

It was sad.

Reality is, it's just a name to those who don't have a relationship with Jesus Christ. It's meaningless if you don't know God. His name doesn't hold power for unbelievers. Just like those who use His name in vain. They don't realize the power is right there at their fingertips. All they have to do is believe.

The name of Jesus is like a weapon. A spiritual one. He wished everyone knew Him like he did.

Most don't.

Most think it's about a bunch of head knowledge. You can graduate from a top Bible college and still not know Jesus. You can even be a pastor and have no idea what salvation means.

Boone saw it a lot. So many people go to church thinking they are doing their duty. They volunteer in different ministries. They call themselves a Christian because they follow all the rules. They think they have to work hard to earn their salvation. That's not what salvation is.

If you don't know Jesus, you're missing the point.

His Aunt Sally told him she was like that most of her life. She told him she was just going through the motions, thinking she had to earn her way to heaven.

She went to church, tithed, and volunteered in several committees. She did all the right things. But in the end, it took her sister's dying for her to understand who Jesus really is.

Why? Because she didn't have a relationship with him. She was missing that. He was glad she came to her senses.

Like he told Kelly, just talk to Him. Tell Him everything.

Which reminded him, Kelly was pretty quiet. He thought she'd say something by now. Sure, he told her to rest, but she was barely moving now. He observed her breathing. *Good!* She was still alive.

The poor girl was exhausted, more like passed out from the trauma. If someone didn't come looking for them soon, she wouldn't make it.

Not only did she have hypothermia, but her broken bones needed attention, and he was sure she had a concussion.

He probably shouldn't let her sleep.

He'd wake her up in a minute. Right now, Boone just wanted

to close his eyes for a second. He was so tired. He could barely keep his eyes open.

Jesus, you know me. I always tell it like it is. If you don't send someone soon, we aren't gonna make it.

He closed his eyes, just for a minute. His wrist burned and ached, the one the birds got. He had every intention of taking care of it, but he couldn't keep his eyes open.

He breathed heavily, feeling drowsy like he was drugged. Boy, he knew he was tired, but this was ridiculous. It was like the energy was being sucked right out of him.

And it was.

Blood spilled from the ripped artery, all over the sand.

FIND ME

Was it a bird?

Kelly lay there, blurry-eyed, half-conscious on the sand. Light rain pelted her face, but that wasn't what woke her. It was something hovering above that caught her attention.

Wind was whipping sand in her face as the object came closer. The loud whirring sound alarmed her. Was she dreaming?

Was it Jesus? She wanted to see his beautiful face again. Did this mean that she died? Did this mean she was in heaven like before, when she was under the water?

Boone! Where was Boone? She rolled her head to the side and saw him sleeping beside her. "Boone?" she squeaked with a raspy voice, but he didn't respond.

Then a figure approached.

"My name is Bo, I'm a First Responder from the U.S Coast Guard Search and Rescue. We're here to help," the husky voice told her.

Kelly tried to respond, but she was so tired. Her mouth wouldn't move properly. The guy tugged at her and checked her body. He patted her down while two other people held her head like a brace.

What were they doing?

"Ma'am, you've got some broken bones. We're going to stabilize your leg and foot before we move you to the stretcher."

They put something on her leg and foot, then they wrapped it up. They did the same with her hand. Suddenly, two of them moved her body to a board and put a cervical collar on her and taped her head securely to the board.

She knew what they were doing. They were saving her. They had finally found her. *Them.* Where was Boone? She couldn't see him now with this thing on her neck. *Boone?*

All she could hear was a team working on him. They were spending a lot of time with him. He was only sleeping, wasn't he? Why wasn't he moving? Why wasn't he responding to them? *Boone?*

The team assessed them like they did her, but she could tell they were more concerned with him than her. "We gotta take him to the chopper, NOW!"

Why? What was happening?

Kelly lay there in the mist, waiting. Waiting. Hadn't that been what she was doing this whole time? What took them so long to find them?

"Is he okay?" she whispered. But nobody heard her. They were all working over there, in the medivac. *Boone?*

Lord, please take care of him.

Warm tears stung as they escaped the corners of her eyes. She looked into the mist and inhaled the cold air. Every breath hurt. As she became more coherent, she realized this was the miracle they were praying for.

They had found them.

Suddenly, Bo and another man came for her stretcher. "Are there any more survivors?" he asked her.

She tried to shake her head to say no, but she couldn't. She blinked against the tears and spoke as loudly as she could. "No!"

That was hard to say.

They lifted her in the chopper and felt the propellers whir. The team continued to work on Boone as the chopper rose into the air. All she could hear were beeps and monitors going off.

They were using a portable defibrillator on him, shocking him. *My God, save this man I love!*

Beeps and monitors continued to go off, and Kelly continued to pray under her breath. She prayed during the whole flight until they touched down in Juneau.

They rushed Boone out first, then her. They ran with his

gurney down a hall and put her in a room in the opposite direction.

After that, everything else was a blur.

When she woke up, she had a cast on her left leg from her knee down to her ankle. Her hand was bandaged with two splints on her broken fingers. Her right arm had a cast from her elbow to her wrist, and her head was wrapped in bandages.

She realized nobody even knew she was there. No relatives would come. No friends. She was all alone.

Not even Ted. Not that she even wanted him there.

She was so far away from home, if you could even call it that anymore. It felt so foreign. Toronto seemed a million miles away.

Loneliness crept in. Kelly remembered her act of desperation that started this whole nightmare. She had run from her life of misery, only to run into something much worse.

What am I doing, Lord?

She remembered what Boone said. All she had to do was keep talking to Jesus. That's a relationship. That is what determines the difference between a believer and someone who just has religion.

Thoughts of her Nana came rushing in. All those years she fought her instruction. All those years, she hated her grandmother pushing Christianity on her. Now she knew she was teaching her how to have a relationship with Jesus. Thank you, Nana! She wished she were still alive to tell her how much she appreciated the lessons, especially memorizing Bible verses. *They sure did come in handy!*

More than you know!

A nurse came into her room just then to check on her. She viewed the monitor and adjusted her IV drip. They were giving her saline to hydrate her, and something for the pain. She couldn't feel a thing.

It was glorious.

Kelly watched as the nurse increased her meds. She wondered if she knew anything about Boone. "Excuse me," she whispered, "I was wondering if you could tell me if Boone is okay?"

"Boone? Who's that?"

Her heart sank. Wouldn't they know who he was? Didn't they bring him in at the same time as her?"

"Boone, he came in with me," she said louder, so the nurse knew how important it was for her to find out if he was okay.

"What's his last name. I'll see what I can find out."

"Boone... ah... I don't remember his last name."

"Well then, I can't help you, honey," the nurse told her point-blank. She was hoping for a kinder response, but Kelly let it go.

She racked her brain to think of his last name. How could she forget his last name? *Oh, Lord, what is it?*

The nurse scurried out before she had a chance to think.

Suddenly, someone from the other side of the curtain began to talk to her. It was an older lady in the bed beside her. She sat on the edge of the bed in a hospital gown and pulled the curtain open.

"Moin," the kind old lady greeted her in a foreign language. "Me know Boone. Boone McKenzie. He's Mien Jung."

Kelly's eyes grew wide. "That's right. Boone McKenzie." Now she remembered. Where was that nurse so she could tell her?

"Kind man, big heart! Big red beard too!" the old lady nodded. "Ja! He's Mien Jung. I teach him Plattdeutsch. Is he here?"

Kelly smiled. He knew her, Boone. "Yes! ... but..."

"He helped me," the old lady told him with a smile.

"He helped me, too."

Kelly sat through an hour of Plattdeutsch, and she didn't even know the woman's name. She was so kind and sweet, and she was thrilled to find someone who knew Boone.

But there was only one thing on her mind. She still hadn't heard a word about how Boone was doing.

It was time to find out!

I CAN TELL

A whole day had passed, and nobody would tell her a thing about Boone. Kelly didn't even know if he was dead or alive.

Unless she was family, they couldn't tell her anything.

The old Mennonite lady she shared a room with claimed he was her boy, but that was more of a joke, she figured out later. She wasn't officially family, so they wouldn't tell her either.

She finally found out her name was Mary. Kelly guessed she was the neighbour who cooked Boone the gluten-free perogies. She'd love to try them one day.

In fact, she'd love a plate of them right now. The boring gluten-free meals the hospital provided tasted like cardboard. At least they had a gluten-free menu. Most don't.

Kelly couldn't take it anymore. She couldn't play one more round of cards with Mary. She had to find out about Boone.

"Excuse me, nurse," she tried asking for the umpteenth time, "I need to know how Boone McKenzie is doing. *Please!*"

"We've been over this, ma'am. I can't tell you anything. Only family. And since you and Mary are not related, I can't help you."

This was frustrating.

The nurse left, and they continued playing cards. There was nothing else to do. She sighed, looking out the window to the street below. It was overcast and rainy, just like where they came from.

Kelly didn't want to think about that.

Those memories were still too painful. Without Boone to calm her down, she couldn't force herself to relive what happened.

Only God knew.

For some reason, Kelly felt distant from God right now. It seemed like he wasn't listening. She prayed all day for Boone to be okay, but still had no answers. Was that God's fault? Probably not, yet sadness consumed her.

Talk to God, Boone said.

She sighed and told Mary she needed to rest. She did really, but mostly she needed some time to process all this. It was too much. It was way too much.

Okay, God. I'm listening. What do you want to tell me?

She and Boone discussed this on one of their talks. He told her, sometimes, when you feel like God is far away, it's then that he wants you to listen. She wondered what that meant.

The Bible. He told her God speaks through his word.

Kelly eyed the Bible on the nightstand beside her bed. She leaned over, wincing in pain, and picked it up.

Where should she start?

She decided to open it at random and see what God had to say to her. Maybe it worked that way. She was about to find out.

It opened to the book of John. Boone said that was a good place to start. She ran her finger down the page and stopped at John 14:27 and read it silently.

"Peace I leave with you: my peace I give you. I do not give to you as the world gives. Do not let your hearts be troubled and do not be afraid."

Peace, that's what she needed. Kelly realized her heart was so troubled that she couldn't calm down. *Okay, Jesus. I hear you. You said you give me peace. I accept that. Boone said to just believe. So, I'm going to believe it all. You gave me peace, so I will try to be peaceful!*

As for the rest of the passage, she wasn't supposed to let her heart be troubled or afraid. That was a hard one. She doubted anyone would be successful at that. Yet, it's what God commanded. Again, if she was going to believe one thing, she had to believe it all. It was a choice. *Okay, God, I will try to do that too.*

The only thing she didn't really understand was the part

that said, *"I do not give to you as the world gives."* What on earth did that mean?

Perhaps the world represents bad things, sinful things. So, if God gives us peace, the world gives us sorrow. Maybe that's what it meant. She had her share of sorrow in the last few days. She let sadness consume her. It was time to stop that. She wanted peace, not sadness from what the world brings. She decided she was choosing *that!*

Lord, help me, Jesus!

Kelly looked out at the rain and smiled. It can either make her happy or sad. She decided she was choosing happiness. She held the Bible to her chest and decided to trust the Lord with whatever happens next.

She closed her eyes and rested, shutting out the world and all its sounds. A hospital is a busy place, and it can become overwhelming with all the beeping of equipment. She didn't have to let it bother her. She could rest in perfect peace.

As Kelly lay there silent, someone interrupted and knocked on the door. It was a nurse she hadn't seen before. "Are you Kelly Preston?" she asked.

"Yes."

"You have a visitor."

Kelly didn't know anyone here. She wondered who would come to see her. She hoped it wasn't Ted or anyone from his family. Yet, the thought of having a visitor excited her, even if it was from someone less desirable. "Who is it?"

Then, a petite native lady emerged from the doorway. She looked to be in her sixties with salt and pepper hair. "Hello? Are you Kelly?"

"Yes, that's me."

"My name is Sally."

Kelly perked up, "As in...Aunty Sally?"

"Aa!"

"Boone! Is he alive?" she asked, hoping it wasn't bad news.

Kelly searched the Tlingit woman's facial expression for a positive answer. The woman smiled widely and nodded, "Aa! He sent me to you."

Kelly burst into tears.

Mary yelped from behind the curtain, eavesdropping on the conversation. "Mien Jung! He strong man!"

"Is he okay?" Kelly asked, wiping tears from her cheeks. "Tell me what's been happening. They wouldn't give me any information."

"Well, my dear, they wouldn't tell him about you either. He was quite worried. He wanted me to find you. I've never seen him like this before."

"Like what?"

"You must mean a lot to him. He's head over heels."

Kelly blushed. She knew exactly what she meant. She tried to hide her emotions, but she couldn't. Her split lip quivered as she said her feelings out loud. "I love him!"

Shouts of joy immediately burst through the curtain again. "Sorry, me bad!" Mary was eavesdropping, but Kelly didn't care. She laughed instead, wiping her eyes.

"I can tell," Aunt Sally winked.

Kelly blushed again.

"Well, first things first, then. He was touch-and-go when they brought him in, but he's doing much better today. They had to give him a blood transfusion. The arteries in his wrist were pretty ripped up. He lost a lot of blood and went into hypovolemic shock."

"But he's going to be okay?"

"Yes! I prayed for a miracle."

"Me too!"

"When can I see him?"

"That, I don't know. I don't think I can keep him away from you for long. As soon as the doctor clears him, he'll be down for sure. They have to take him off the monitors first. I can't believe what you guys went through. He told me the whole horrific story. I'm so sorry! You both are lucky to be alive. We've been looking for you for days!"

Yes, they were lucky to be alive! Though luck had nothing to do with it, she knew what she meant. *It was all Jesus!*

"So...did he tell you about the-the...*creatures?*"

"He didn't have to. *I guessed.* I could see it on his face, and I can see it on yours too. My people call it the *Kooshdaa kaa.* We know the legends. I'm so sorry that happened to you!"

Kelly's mind reeled with the horror of it all. How it killed Parker was so barbaric. How it almost killed them was still disturbing. She tried to hold back tears, but she couldn't. She started to sob uncontrollably.

"Hey-hey! I'm sorry, I didn't mean to upset you."

"It's okay...I-I guess I'm still in shock!"

"Oh, you poor thing," Aunt Sally tried to console her.

It didn't take much to upset her these days. Kelly figured it would be a long road to recovery. At least she wouldn't have to do it alone. That brought her comfort. She had God and she had Boone.

Boy, she sure missed that man. She missed everything about him. He could brighten a room with just his smile. Boone McKenzie was a legend. His ex-girlfriend was right about that. He was unforgettable.

Then, a knock at the door interrupted her thoughts. A nurse she hadn't seen before came to the door. This was becoming Grand Central Station today. *What next?*

"Excuse me!" the nurse smiled, "You have another visitor. Someone's been very eager to see you."

"*Boone!*"

"How's my *Kells-Bells?*" he blurted out as they wheeled him in.

"YOU'RE ALIVE! she shrieked, wiggling off the bed one-legged. She pushed her aching body to embrace him, bawling like a blubbering fool. "I THOUGHT YOU WERE DEAD!"

"ME? No way! You can't get rid of me that easily!"

Aunt Sally pulled up a chair for her, and she sat facing him as Boone held both her hands in his. They paused, pressing foreheads together in silence. The pain was real, and the memories strong.

Nobody knew what it was really like to almost have your soul sucked out of you. Kelly couldn't even put it into words. It was indescribable. It was something only she and Boone shared.

Maybe it should stay that way.

From the beginning of her journey, she'd been running. No matter what, she couldn't escape her life. She couldn't ignore that her father abandoned her and left scars so deep they destroyed every relationship she ever had...*except the one with Jesus!*

He tore down the wall.

She didn't even realize she had a wall until now. She was always protecting herself from being hurt. A little girl with a father wound always does. If you're not careful, that kind of trauma can destroy your soul, *literally!*

Kelly understood that now.

God used the trauma she went through to heal her soul. He taught her what it meant to be vulnerable and open up her heart. It wasn't until she did that, that He was able to teach her how to have a relationship with Him. He was able to show her how a loving father protects a child through everything.

Like it should be.

And now, as she gazed at her ginger lumberjack, she realized he was part of the journey all along. Through healing comes opportunity, and opportunity was Boone McKenzie. She hoped the next chapter would lead to much better days...*with him in her life.*

"Earth to Kelly!" Boone joked, "You look like you're a million miles away."

"No, just thinking."

"I hope it's about me," he winked.

"Only if you take me on that date you promised!"

Boone leaned in to kiss her. "Sounds like a plan."

The End

HOW TO BECOME A CHRISTIAN

The Bible says we are saved by grace through faith in Jesus Christ. (Ephesians 2:8-9). We don't have to earn our salvation by working for it. Grace Alone. Faith Alone.

Salvation is simple, like the ABCs.

A –ADMIT you are a sinner. "For all have sinned and fall short of the glory of God. (Romans 3:23).

B – BELIEVE in Jesus. "For God so loved the world that he gave his one and only Son, that whoever believes in him shall not perish but have eternal life." (John 3:16).

C – CONFESS that Jesus is your Lord. "If we confess our sins, he is faithful and just and will forgive us our sins and purify us from all unrighteousness." (1 John 1:9).

Romans 10:13 – "Everyone who calls on the name of the Lord will be saved."

The Salvation Prayer

Dear Jesus, I admit that I am a sinner and in need of a Saviour. I believe with all my heart that you are the Son of God who died and rose again for me. You took my punishment, so I don't have to. You made me clean by your finished work on the cross. Today, I acknowledge that salvation is not of my own doing, but is by grace through faith alone. It is a free gift to me, and I accept that gift. You are my Lord and Saviour forever! Thank you!

Congratulations!

If you prayed this prayer and you believe it with all your heart, you are now a believer! Remember to talk to him every day. That's how you have a relationship with Him. His spirit will guide you and help you!

Follow Him all the days of your life!

ABOUT THE AUTHOR

Kathleen Morris is a Christian author of Evangelical fiction, both in romantic suspense and thrillers. She loves to write about Biblical truths and show how her characters find Christ through traumatic circumstances. She writes for ministry and loves the art of storytelling. Kathleen makes her home in Saskatchewan, Canada, and loves spending time with her husband, children and grandchildren. It is her hope and dream to be used by God to spread the gospel through her writing.

For more books by Kathleen Morris, go to her Amazon author page.